Tl

The

God

Whistle

Ralph Nelson Willett

Ralph Nelson Willett

Can I Ask A Favor?

If you enjoy this book, please consider providing a review on Amazon for it. Reviews help readers decide if they would like to purchase a book or not and is useful for the author when making decisions on what to write for his next book.

Here's the link where you can add your review:
www.NorthernOvationMedia.com/thegodwhistle/review

Thank you.

Want Free Books?

From time to time the author offers his Kindle books for free to those who are interested. These offers are highly temporary. If you'd like to know when you can get his books for free, please sign up for his mailing list at:
www.NorthernOvationMedia.com/freebooks

~~~~

The God Whistle

Ralph Nelson Willett

Ralph Nelson Willett

Chapter 1

"The timing could be better," Mary said as she stood in front of the full-length mirror. She held the bridesmaid gown under her chin. Smoothing out the wrinkles, she pressed the dress tightly against herself.

"I can't say I'm a big fan of Friday night weddings," Adam said as he adjusted the length of his tie.

"It was the only time they could get the reception hall," Mary replied. She twisted side to side, examining herself in the mirror. "Remember how hard it was for us, last minute and all?" She swayed, letting the dress swing side to side. "Ash could have done a lot worse with picking out the dresses," Mary told him. "At least these aren't ugly."

Adam stepped up behind her and wrapped his arms around her waist. He kissed the nape of her neck and nuzzled in. "Just remember," he said, "you're not supposed to be more beautiful than the bride. You might have to tone it down a bit."

Mary leaned into him. Holding the bridesmaid dress to her with one hand, she used her free hand to pull his head in closer to her. "You're sweet, Babe," she told him as she turned her head and kissed him. He looked good in a suit, and she was excited to be out with him tonight even if they would have the kids with them. "You look good, too," she told him. "You should wear a suit more often."

"For you, Babe, anytime." He kissed the nape of her neck again as he began slowly swaying her back and forth. "I think we got some dancing to do tonight."

"Hmmmm," she hummed. "I think we do." They remained swaying together in front of the mirror with his arms wrapped around her from behind. "I suspect that I'm going to be pretty tired tonight so don't get your hopes up," she said recognizing Adam's nonverbal hints. She felt Adam instantly tense and relax again. He loosened his arms and ballooned his cheeks as he blew out a breath. Releasing her, he pivoted and stepped away.

"How are the kids coming?" Mary asked as she stepped away from the mirror.

"They're all ready," he replied. "They're out in the living room playing. Aric isn't enthused about going."

"He'll have fun," Mary told him. "He's never been to a wedding and reception before. How's Kara coming?"

"She's a little princess in her dress, and she knows it. She's playing with her doll."

"OK," Mary said as she held the dress up by its hanger. "I'll put this in the car, and we can go. You ready?"

"Just waiting on you, Babe," he replied with enthusiasm.

Mary carried the dress into the garage along with a small makeup bag and shoes and placed them in the trunk of the car. When she returned inside the house, she found Adam standing at the door holding their three-year-old daughter. Kara had a terrified look on her face. Adam looked disgusted. Kara had just vomited down the front of his suit. He held his free arm out to his side trying to distance himself from it.

Kara began to cry.

"Ewwwwwww," yelled Aric as he ran toward his room. "Kara threw up!"

"Oh, maaaaannnn," Adam said as he examined himself and Kara.

Mary ran up to Kara and took her from Adam's arms. Kara's dress was soiled. "Oh, come on, Sweetie," she told Kara as she rushed her toward the bathroom. She sat Kara down on the counter and began to clean her up with a washcloth. Kara cried loudly. "It's OK, Honey.

It's OK," Mary said trying to console her. She removed the soiled dress and tossed it onto the hamper lid. Picking Kara up again, she gave her a hug as Kara began to calm down.

"I threw up, Mommy," Kara whimpered.

"I know, Sweetie," Mary told her. "I know. You're OK."

Adam stepped into the bathroom. He had removed his suit jacket and shirt and was wearing only his T-shirt. "It's a good thing this happened *before* we left for the wedding," he said.

"What are we going to do?" Mary asked him. "Do you think your Mother would watch her?"

"They're out tonight at a business dinner Dad's got. That doesn't leave us with a lot of choices. What about your sister, Rhonda?"

"She's working. That means you'll have to stay home with her. I can't miss the wedding. I'm in it."

"I know," he said. "I'll stay home with Kara and Aric."

"Ohhhhh," she whined. "I was looking forward to dancing with you tonight."

"Not gonna happen. Sorry about that," Adam said as he took Kara from her. "You need to go. I've got this."

"OK," Mary replied. "I'll text you just before I leave for home."

"Yeah. OK. Watch what you drink. You're driving," he reminded her.

"No problem." She checked the clock on the kitchen stove as she walked past the kitchen to the door. She had lost ten minutes while tending to Kara. "I'm sorry," she told Adam as she kissed him goodbye.

"Kids," he replied with a forced smile. "What you gonna do?" He leaned in again and gave her another kiss. "Have fun."

"I will," she told him as she walked out into the garage, keys in hand. Adam closed the door behind her.

~~~~~

Friends and family members of the bride and groom were all seated. The wedding party lined up by twos behind closed doors at the rear of the sanctuary. The twin flower girls waited to one side beside their mother. They giggled nervously at each other. Each held baskets of rose petals. Mary thought they could not have been more than five years old, but they waited patiently and looked pretty in their white dresses.

Each of the four bridesmaids paired up with a groomsman. Gabe Fellows stood beside her. She had not seen Gabe since high school. Unremarkable then, he had filled out into an athletic build that seemed to be perfect for the black tuxedo he wore. His eyes sparkled, and he smiled brightly. He appeared confident and at ease. Although she remembered having a few classes with him in High School, she could not remember anything else about him. There was nothing in her memories of him that stood out. He was just another boy that happened to go to the same small school as she did.

Mary held the bouquet of flowers to her nose, closed her eyes and inhaled the fresh floral aroma.

"Nice?" asked Gabe standing beside her.

"Oh yeah," she replied without letting down the flowers. "I love that smell." She tilted the flowers toward him. "Wanna smell?"

"Sure," he said smiling. Mary held the flowers up, and Gabe leaned in and inhaled deeply.

"Oh yeah," he said as he stood straight again. "That is nice."

Mary watched as he looked down and smiled at the twins in their fluffy white dresses. "You married, Gabe?"

"No, I'm not," he answered. "I just haven't found the right woman yet, I suppose." He shrugged his shoulders. "It just never worked out."

"So, you dating anyone?"

"Not at the moment. I broke up with someone about two months ago, but we weren't that serious. What about you?

"Married ten years now," she answered. "Two kids."

"Is your family here with you?" he asked.

The music changed, and the doors to the sanctuary opened, interrupting their conversation. Mary hooked her arm into Gabe's. Rows of people twisted in their seats to see them standing in the doorway. Two ushers unrolled a satin runner down the aisle.

Mary and Gabe were signaled. Arm in arm they began a slow walk up the aisle. Upon reaching the altar, Mary unhooked her arm from Gabe. Gabe bowed his head to her and took his place to the right as Mary took her place to her left.

After all of the bridesmaids and groomsmen took their places, the groom and minister emerged from a side door and took their places. As the twins then began their walk slowly towards the front, the doors closed behind them. The girls tossed rose from small wicker baskets they held onto the satin runner. Cameras lit the sanctuary with flashes capturing their smiles.

When the twins reached the front, one stood by the maid of honor who placed her hand on the little girl's shoulder. The second twin stood beside her sister and held her hand.

The music changed again. The sanctuary doors opened again, revealing the bride arm in arm with her father. Everyone stood and turned to face her.

Ashlee wore a long white satin wedding dress that trailed behind her on the white satin carpet runner. She held a large bouquet in front of her. A thin veil covered her face. Cameras began flashing with renewed vigor as she and her father walked the aisle slowly. They stopped in front of the minister and waited for the music to stop.

"Who gives this woman to be wed to this man?" asked the minister.

"Her mother and I," replied her father. He then stepped back and let the groom take his place beside her.

~~~

After completing the ceremony and greeting the guests, the wedding party returned to the sanctuary for more pictures. When the photographer had finished with the formal poses, they went out to the large limousine waiting for them in front of the church. The limousine driver led a procession through town with nearly twenty cars following behind them, blaring their horns.

Pulling up at the reception hall, everyone exited the limousine and entered the front door in pairs. A groomsman escorted each bridesmaid. Gabe stepped out first. Mary hooked her arm into Gabe's as they entered. He escorted her to her seat at the end of the head table and then took his place on the groom's side.

Each bridesmaid and groomsman entered the building to a light applause. When the bride and groom entered the applause turned thunderous as everyone stood to welcome them.

As the dinner wrapped up, the band began to play at the far end of the hall. Gabe stepped over to the bridesmaid's end of the table. "Ladies, can I get you anything to drink from the bar? I'm buying," he told them.

"Sure," said the maid of honor, already knowing it was an open bar. "Thank you. I'd like another white wine please."

"OK," Gabe said.

"I'll have a white wine too, please," the second bridesmaid told him with a smile.

"Melissa?" Gabe prompted.

"Beer," Melissa said. "See if they have White Lake Brown Cream Ale."

"And if they don't?" Gabe asked her.

"Then a Blue Moon."

Gabe turned to Mary. "And what would you like?" he asked her.

"I'm driving, but I think I can handle one more. I'll take a white wine, please."

Gabe repeated the orders back as he pointed to each one of them in turn. "White wine, white wine, White Lake Brown Cream Ale, white wine." He then nodded to Melissa sitting next to Mary, "and if they don't have White Lake then a Blue Moon."

"Thanks, Gabe," said the maid of honor loudly over the din of the hall.

Mary turned to Melissa. "What's White Lake Brown Cream Ale?" she asked.

"It's a beer. A brown ale. I love it," Melissa told her. "Have you ever tried a cream beer?"

"Never heard of it."

"It's good. You should try it."

"I'm driving tonight, so I think this will be my last one," Mary replied.

"That's too bad. You could be having a bit of fun. Too bad your husband couldn't make it. You'll miss out on all the good dances."

"I know it," Mary grinned back. "I may have to hijack one of the kids around here to dance with me. I was looking forward to it."

The God Whistle

Melissa and Mary had become close friends not long after Ashlee had introduced them to each other a year earlier. Recently married, Melissa had moved to town to be with her husband. She taught social studies at the high school. Since Mary taught at the junior high, they felt a common bond.

Gabe returned holding a small tray with three glasses of white wine and a glass filled to a foaming top with a dark brown beer. He set the tray down on the table and handed out the drinks.

As Gabe passed the beer glass to Melissa, she handed it off to Mary. "Mary, you take this one. I'll drink the wine for now. I'd like you to try this. It's good." Gabe raised an eyebrow, looked at Melissa and then back at Mary.

"OK," Mary tentatively replied as she took the beer from her. She looked up at Gabe. "Gabe if I don't like this then you'll have to go get me another white."

He hesitated a moment, grinned and said, "No problem." He handed the white wine to Melissa. "Enjoy," he said smiling back at Mary as he walked back to his seat.

Mary took a tentative sip of the White Lake Brown Cream Ale Beer. "OK," she told Melissa, mildly surprised. "I'm not a beer drinker, but I have to admit that's good," she said as she raised her glass to eye level so she could peer into it.

"I told you," Melissa said as she tilted her wine glass toward the beer. "That's good beer. I discovered it in New York when Cary and I went last year."

"Is Cary here tonight?"

"Nope. He's in Denver for work. I'm flying solo this evening, too."

"So, who are *you* going to dance with?" Mary asked her.

"Maybe I'll hijack one of the kids, too," she replied grinning, at her.

Halfway through the White Lake beer, Mary leaned over to Melissa tilting her glass toward her. "This stuff is strong. I can feel it already," she told her.

"I know. It's good, right?" Melissa asked smiling. "But it's not *that* strong. You must not be a big drinker."

"I'm not," Mary replied.

The MC announced that it was time for the first dance. The bride and groom stepped onto the dance floor. The band began playing a song that Mary was not familiar with but she enjoyed watching the couple dance. The MC then asked for the father of the bride to dance with his daughter and for the groom to dance with her mother. Mary gulped the last of the beer just as the MC asked that the wedding party join the bride and groom on the dance floor. Gabe stepped over to Mary and held out his arm for her. He smiled broadly at her with glistening eyes.

Mary took his arm and stood. She was starting to feel energized at the thought of dancing. With Gabe walking beside her, she danced her way to the floor. The song was a slow one, and they danced slowly to it. She wanted something more upbeat, but they swayed together as Gabe held her gently by the waist.

"I can't wait to get this party started," Mary told Gabe.

"Neither can I," he replied. "Where's your husband tonight?"

"He couldn't make it. He's home with the kids," she said. Then she added as she looked up into his face grinning broadly, "he'll be fine without me for once."

"Well, you just may have to be my dance partner tonight then," Gabe told her.

"Dancing," she said as she raised her arms above her head and arched backward in Gabe's arms. He swung her around in a tight loop before she stood straight again. "I love to dance. We can dance, but they gotta play something faster."

"I'm sure they will," Gabe responded.

Mary could feel the energy surging through her at the thought of dancing, but she pulled herself tightly into Gabe and laid her head on his shoulder for the remainder of the slow dance. He pulled her in tighter and held her there as they swayed until the music ended.

"OK," the MC announced. "All dance!"

The music picked up to a faster beat. "Yes!" Mary exclaimed as she pulled Gabe by the hand to the center of the dance floor. She began dancing to the beat of the music with her arms in the air. Closing her eyes, she swayed back and forth in rhythmic gyrations. Gabe danced in front of her at a more moderate pace as he watched her.

They danced to a second song and then a third. Sweat beaded on her forehead. When the music paused for a moment between songs Gabe leaned in and asked, "Can I get you another drink?"

The music began with a song at a slower pace. Mary looked up into Gabe's face, pressed herself up against him and clasped her hand around his neck. She began swaying to the music again as she stared up into his eyes.

"Can I get you another drink?" he asked again.

"Not yet," she answered just loud enough to hear. "I'm not thirsty."

Sweat began running down her cheek. She leaned her head onto her shoulder and wiped it dry with the fabric of her gown. "This is fun. I like dancing. I could dance all night," she told Gabe.

"It looks like you can," he replied. "But you need to drink some water or something."

"After this dance," she replied as she buried her head into his shoulder again.

The music ended and started again with another upbeat song. "Oh, yeah," she said loudly as she began her gyrations again. Gabe stepped in and pulled her by the arm off the dance floor. As they crossed the wooden floor to the carpeted floor, Mary stopped, refusing to move further. "What's the matter with you?" she asked him incredulously.

"We've got to get some more liquid in you before you dehydrate."

"I'm not thirsty," she protested.

"Look," he said sternly as if talking to a child. "I'm thirsty, so you've got to be thirsty. Come with me. We'll get something to drink. Then we can dance some more."

Reluctantly she let him guide her by the hand to the bar and asked the bartender for two more beers. Mary kept her eyes on the dance floor as she bounced. Gabe had to brush her arm with the beer glass to get her to look down and take it. They stood off to one side as they drank their beers. Mary drank hers in several quick swallows, spilling some down her cheek. She giggled as she wiped her mouth with her hand and looked at Gabe. He smiled at her.

"Hurry up," she told him. "More dancing!"

Gabe hurried to finish his beer and then let himself be led by Mary back to the dance floor. They began dancing again just as the song ended.

Mary whined in disappointment as the MC announced it was time for the cutting of the cake. Both Mary and Gabe returned to their places at the table. The bride and groom posed at the cake table for the cameras, cut a small piece and fed it to each other. Glasses began to ring out as the guests began to tap the sides of their glasses with their silverware. Everyone cheered as the bride and groom kissed.

"Hey," Melissa said as she leaned in getting Mary's attention. Mary looked at her with wild eyes and a big smile. "How much have you had to drink?"

"Just some beer."

"How many?" Melissa asked.

"Just the wine with dinner and that beer you gave me."

"Well, you look like you've had too much."

Mary blinked heavily at her. "Nah," she replied. "I'm fine. Why would you think I'm drunk?"

"Because of the way you're dancing and hanging all over Gabe. You need to lay off the drinks for a while."

The smile fell away from Mary's face. "I'm fine. I haven't had too much to drink. I'm just feeling good because I get to dance for once."

"Maybe you better dance with someone else for a while before you embarrass yourself with Gabe."

Mary was beginning to become angry. "It's none of your business who I dance with. I'm fine."

"Mary," she said pointing to her with her open hand. "Look at you. You look like you've had too much tonight already. You still need to drive home."

Mary blinked heavily at her again. Her eyes went out of focus and felt as if they had crossed. She took a moment and retrained her vision as she looked at Melissa. Mary swore harshly. "I said I'm fine. I'm just dancing. You can leave me alone. It's none of your business."

Melissa leaned away, shocked at having been sworn at by Mary. They stared at each other for a moment. Mary gazed at her oddly. Melissa relaxed. "OK, Mary," she said in a quiet tone. "But promise me you won't have anything more to drink."

Mary tilted her head. "I'm not promising anything."

"Please," Melissa pleaded again. "You have to drive home. If you need me to, I can drive you home."

Mary leaned in close and then signaled Melissa to lean in so she could talk to her quietly. Melissa leaned in and turned an ear to her. "It's none of your business," Mary said in a loud whisper. Melissa leaned away from her, the hurt on her face was evident. She stared into Mary's face as Mary continued to lean in toward her blinking heavily. After a moment Melissa stood and walked away. Mary sat straight in her chair. Her anger quickly faded. She raised her hands again and gyrated in her chair mimicking moves made earlier on the dance floor.

Gabe walked over to her with a glass of water and handed it to Mary. "What's this?" she asked.

"Water. Drink," he ordered with a smile. "You're starting to look dehydrated."

Mary took a swallow and set the glass down. "Drink," Gabe demanded.

"OK… OK…," Mary said as she lifted the glass to her lips. She eyed him defiantly as she drank the glass empty. She set it down hard. "There! You happy now?" Her words slurred slightly.

"Yes. Thank you," replied Gabe. He began to walk away, and Mary stopped him.

"Hey!" she said a bit too loudly as she pointed at him. "Next dance is mine."

Gabe turned to face her, smiled broadly and gave her a thumbs up. He walked to his seat at the opposite end of the head table.

The MC asked for all the single women to gather on the dance floor. The bride stood in front of them and tossed her bouquet over her shoulder. The crowd burst into a loud cheer as one of the women caught it.

Mary watched from her seat at the table. Her energy was nearly uncontrollable as she bounced in her chair. After several minutes, the band started up again, and Mary nearly sprinted over to Gabe and dragged him to the floor.   The dancing continued as she gyrated smoothly in front of Gabe who still danced at a much slower pace. He appeared to be amused.

"Thanks, Gabe," she said to him over the music.

"For what?" he asked.

"Dancing with me." She gyrated down into a low squat and returned upright as she fluffed her hair.

"No problem," Gabe replied. "I love to dance."

A brief pause came between songs. Gabe leaned in and asked, "Can I get you another beer?"

"Yes!" She replied, "One of those White Lake beers."

"Sure. You stay here and dance. I'll be right back."

The music started again. Gabe walked toward the bar as Mary began her solo dance near the edge of the dance floor. Gabe returned before the song ended and stood just off the dance floor holding the two beers. He sipped one as he watched Mary dance. She saw him standing at the edge of the dance floor and focused the attention of her dance on him. Her dancing was beginning to become more seductive. It made him smile.

Mary stepped over to him as the song ended and took her beer. She drank it quickly and handed the glass back to him. She was sweating profusely. The music started again, and she stepped back on the floor as she waved her arms in the air. Gabe set her empty glass and the remainder of his beer on the nearest empty guest table and joined her on the floor.

As Gabe joined her in the dance, she stepped in close enough to rub against him as she danced. Gabe's look of amusement broadened as he looked her in the eyes. Mary's energy seemed to be fading quickly as her gyrations slowed. Her dancing appeared to transform into something even more seductive as she focused her dance on Gabe.

The music changed to a slow dance. Gabe stepped in to hold Mary, and he wrapped his arms around her waist. He pulled her in tightly. Together they gyrated in a slow rhythm as Mary rested her head on his shoulder with her eyes closed.

Mary seemed to calm herself as she held onto Gabe. Nearly halfway through the song, Gabe tilted his head back to look at her. The motion caused Mary to lean back and look at him. Her eyes glistened at him. She blinked several times as she tried to bring him into focus. Gabe leaned in and kissed her on the forehead. Mary rested her head on his shoulder again. They danced only moments longer before Gabe kissed her on her head again. He put a finger under her chin and lifted it to face him. Gabe kissed her on the forehead a third time. Mary made no attempt to avoid it. He then loosened his grip from around her waist and leaned in to kiss her on the mouth. Again, Mary did not try to avoid it. Gabe leaned back to look in her eyes. She was beginning to look tired as her energy drained from her. He leaned in and kissed her again with a deepening passion. Mary returned his passion with her own as they stood kissing on the dance floor. Gabe pulled back from the kiss again and resumed the slow dance. Mary rested her head on his shoulder again with her eyes closed. Reaching around her, he placed one hand on her buttocks and pulled her in tightly. Mary did not react. She let him hold her tightly against him.

The music ended, and they separated. "I'm getting tired," Mary told him.

"No doubt," Gabe replied. "You've been dancing all night." He took her by the arm, and she leaned against his shoulder as he walked her off the floor. He directed her toward the vestibule, and they stepped out. They stepped a few feet in and out of view of the doorway. Gabe turned Mary to face him. She looked up at him blankly. A smile spread across his face. He tugged lightly at her arm. Mary nearly fell into him as she stepped in to embrace him. Gabe lifted her chin again and kissed her deeply. She tightened her arms around his neck as their kiss deepened.

The passion lasted several moments before being interrupted. "Mary! Can I talk to you?" Melissa's voice caused Mary to pull away from the kiss. Mary leaned back into Gabe's arms as she turned to face her. She blinked hard twice and struggled to bring Melissa into focus.

"What?" Mary asked breathlessly.

"Can I talk to you for a minute?"

"What?" she asked again.

Melissa stepped in closer, ignoring Gabe.

"Mary, you're married. You shouldn't be doing this," Melissa told her.

Mary leaned her head against Gabe. "Leave me alone. I'm fine." ▪Her words slurred.

"You shouldn't be doing this," she said again as she stepped closer.

Mary stiff-armed her and swore at her. "Leave me alone, Melissa. I'm fine." She closed her eyes for a moment, took a deep breath and let it out as she opened her eyes again to look at Melissa.

Melissa stood back seemingly stunned. Mary turned back to Gabe and leaned up for another kiss. Gabe cupped a hand behind her head and held her as he kissed her with an open mouth. He turned her to face the door. She held his arm and leaned on his shoulder as they walked out together.

Chapter 2

Mary awoke hungover and feeling out of place. She tried to orient herself. Light leaked in from around unfamiliar drapes. There was enough light to recognize she was not in her own room. ·She turned to her left and gasped as she saw Gabe on his side, staring at her.

"Good morning," he said gently.

"Gabe!" she said as panic began to set in. She sat straight up in bed and realized that she was completely naked.

"Gabe!" she said again. She looked around the darkened room and found the clock with its blue-green numbers. Nine-fifteen. The time increased her panic. She swore. Mary looked around to try and find her clothing in the darkened room. She turned on a lamp next to the bed and saw her clothes thrown haphazardly on a chair.

In a rush, she jumped out of the bed and began dressing as quickly as possible. Gabe watched her, grinning. "You were awesome," he said.

"Gabe...," Mary said.

"Hey," he continued as he watched her dress, "I know you're married and all but can I see you again?"

"No!" she replied. "This was a mistake." She swore again. "This should not have happened."

Gabe sat up and put his feet on the floor. "What are you talking about?" he asked. "Last night was awesome!"

"No... Gabe..." She looked around the room and recognized it as a hotel room. She swore again. "I've got to get home."

Gabe dressed casually as he watched Mary quickly throwing on her clothes. "We could hang out for a while," he told her.

"No! I have to get home," Mary repeated. "My husband is going to kill me."

"Well if he does, come see me. We're good together."

"Gabe! No!" she said as she slipped into her bridesmaid gown. "I'm sorry. I didn't mean for this to happen. I'm married."

"Well he's a lucky man," he said with a smirk.

Mary looked frantically for her clutch bag and did not see it. Again, she swore. "All my stuff must still be at the reception hall. I need you to take me back there."

He did not reply but finished getting dressed.

"Gabe?"

"I've got things to do," he said as he pulled his wallet out. "Here's $20 for a cab." He held the bill out toward her.

Mary stared at it blankly for a moment and then turned angry. Quickly she put her shoes on, rushed to the door, unlocked it and left the room. The door closed automatically behind her. The numbers on the door told her she was on the second floor of the motel. She moved quickly down the hall looking for an elevator but found the steps first. She took the stairs rapidly down until she reached the first floor. Panic rose through her. Her breathing became shallow as her eyes scanned the room. She saw the service counter. It had one person behind it speaking with a guest.

Mary rushed to the counter and leaned against it. "Can you call me a cab?"

The man serving the guest looked up at her, surprised at the interruption. "I'll be with you in just a moment, Ma'am."

The older woman checking out looked at Mary. Their eyes met. "Wedding?" the woman asked.

"Yeah," Mary responded tersely.

The man behind the counter handed the woman an envelope and said, "Thank you for staying with us."

"Thank you," the woman said. She turned, gave Mary a smile, took her suitcase by its handle and rolled it away with her toward the door.

"How can I help…," the man began.

"Please," Mary interrupted. "Call me a cab."

The man smirked as he reached for the telephone. "No problem, Ma'am." He made the call and hung up the phone. "It will be about fifteen minutes. They'll meet you at the front door."

She paced nervously outside the front door as she waited. The air was cold. She tried to stay in the early morning sun, trying to let it warm her. After several minutes the cab pulled up, and she sat in the back.

"Florentine Reception Hall," she told the driver.

"Do you have address?" the man asked in a thick European accent.

Mary swore again. "I'm sorry, I don't," she said still trying to push down the panic. "Let me go in and see if they can tell me."

"Please wait. I find," the driver said in broken English. He pulled out his cell phone, selected a contact from his contact list and waited. He spoke again a moment later as he asked the person on the other end of the phone for the address. Seconds later he said, "Thank you" and disconnected the phone.

"I have now," he said over his shoulder toward Mary. "Not far."

"Thank you," she replied.

It only took a few minutes before they reached the reception hall. The driver stopped the meter and said, "Nine dollars and thirty cents."

Mary's distress deepened as she realized she had no money. "I'm sorry," she said, "my purse is in there. Let me get it, and I'll be right back."

"OK," he said as he started the meter again. "I wait."

Mary stepped out of the cab and looked around the parking lot. She saw her car parked near the street side of the parking lot. She had arranged for someone to bring her car and street clothes to the reception hall from the church. Now she only had to find her clothes and keys.

She stepped to the front door and tried to open it. It was locked. She peered inside and could see people cleaning. A woman came to the door after Mary knocked solidly on it.

"We're closed," the woman shouted from behind the door.

"I know," Mary shouted back. "But my clothes and car keys are in there."

The woman unlocked the door, and Mary stepped inside. She did not know where her belongings would have been dropped off. She checked the coat room first and found the duffel bag she had put her clothes in. She opened it up and found her purse and keys inside. She did a quick check to see if her credit cards were still there. She was relieved to see they were.

Nearly running back to the taxi, Mary paid him with her card. She watched as the taxi drove away. Her car was on the far side of the lot. Pulling her keys from her purse, she walked quickly to it.

~~~~

Mary entered the house through the garage door to find Adam sitting at the kitchen table staring angrily at her.

"I'm so sorry," Mary told him. Adam did not respond. "I had way too much to drink last night and ended up staying with Melissa." She had practiced her excuse on the drive home. It was weak, but she hoped it would be enough. "I should have called, I know."

Adam sat leaning forward with his forearms resting on the table. He twirled his cell phone over and over between his hands. His jaw clenched. Mary set her purse on the table and stepped closer to him. Adam now stared straight forward, every muscle taut.

"I'm sorry," she said again.

Adam set the cell phone on the table with its screen up. He unlocked it as Mary watched and opened an email. "$12 for a taxi cab," he said referring to the automatic email sent for each credit card transaction.

"Yeah," Mary replied. "I had to take a cab back to get to my car."

Adam's muscles tensed to the point he was nearly shaking. The veins on his neck were beginning to stand out, and his face was turning red. "That's not the problem," he finally said.

Mary watched him with a growing sense of foreboding. He switched his phone to his message screen and selected a message. Tapping it once a video began to play. She heard dance music. Adam tilted the phone so that it would play full screen. Mary looked closer at the screen. She could see that it was a video of her slow dancing with Gabe. She had her head resting against his chest as he held her tight against him.

Panic began to set in. She remained silent as she watched Adam grow steadily angrier. Adam switched to another video. Again, it was a video of her slow dancing with Gabe. "I'm sorry..." she began.

"Watch!" Adam shouted as he kept focused on the screen. The video continued and showed Mary initiating a passionate kiss with Gabe. The kiss lasted painfully long. Adams' face became crimson.

Mary sat down in the chair directly to Adam's right. "Where did you get this?" she asked.

"Someone sent it to me last night."

"Who?" she asked meekly.

"What does it matter?" he shouted at her. His shouting made her jump. "I've got friends too!"

"Adam, I don't remember any of this. I don't know what happened. I had too much to drink."

His breathing was loud and shallow through his nose. "Oh," he said a little more calmly. "There's more." He switched to another video. The video showed Mary and Gabe passionately kissing in the reception hall vestibule.

"Adam..." Mary tried again.

"Watch!" he shouted again as he shook his cell phone in her direction. She watched as the video showed Melissa confronting her and Mary stiff arming her away. It showed her again initiating a passionate kiss with Gabe as Melissa stood back watching them uncomfortably. The video continued as it showed Gabe directing her out of the door to the parking lot. Whoever had recorded the video followed them at a distance as they walked to

Gabe's car. Gabe opened the door for her and just before she climbed in Gabe initiated another kiss. Mary responded in turn with a passionate embrace. Gabe then directed her into the car, closed the door behind her, climbed in the driver's side and then drove off.

"I don't remember any of this," Mary said as she began to tear up. Adam sat silent. "I'm so sorry. I don't know what happened."

Adam tensed and faced forward. He was shaking. He set the phone down on the table and folded his hands together resting them on the table.

"Adam, I am so sorry," she tried again.

"Shut up!" Adam screamed as he faced her, "Shut up! Shut up! Shut up!"

Mary slid her chair back to add distance between them. His face had turned crimson red with anger. She was afraid of him.

Adam calmed his voice as he fought to control his emotions. "You know what really bothers me?" he asked. "You haven't been *that* passionate with me in years." He jutted his jaw out. He shook with anger as he glared at her.

Mary sank deeper into her chair under Adam's glare and remained silent. She tried to look him in the eye, but the anger she saw there forced her to turn her eyes downward to the floor. Tears flowed down her cheeks. Adam was breathing heavily and loudly through his nostrils. Each inward breath seemed to make the veins in his neck stand out further.

After several moments Adam calmed himself. He faced forward again with his forearms resting on the table. He resumed slowly twirling the cell phone between his hands. The color in his neck and face began to fade.

"Where are the kids?" Mary asked softly without looking at him.

"They're at my mom's house," he replied. The anger in his voice drained away.

"Kara OK?"

"She's fine." The phone spun in his hands.

A long silence remained. Mary held her hands together in her lap as she stared at the floor. Tears ran down her face and fell from her jawline onto her dress. "Adam, I'm..."

"I want you out," he interrupted her.

More silence. "Where am I going to go?" Mary asked weakly.

"I don't care," Adam quietly said. It was almost a whisper. He sat staring at the phone being flipped over and over between his fingers.

Mary waited to see if Adam was going to say more. The only sound was a steady ticking of the kitchen clock and

Adam's breathing. Adam set the phone face down on the table in front of him, placed one hand on top of the other and rested them on the table. His eyes glazed over as they remained fixed on the phone. The anger in his face was fading into sadness.

Mary eventually stood and walked to their bedroom to find that Adam had placed four suitcases for her just inside the door. She closed the door behind her and wiped her eyes. She changed out of the bridesmaid gown and into a pair of jeans and a sweatshirt. She packed the suitcases with what she could fit in them and set them by the door. She then laid out her hanging clothes on the bed. After looking around for what else she may want to take, she opened the bedroom door again and looked out. Adam was still sitting at the table. He had placed his elbows on the table and rested his chin on the back of his hands. He turned slowly to look at her. His jaw was still set tightly, and its muscles stood out. Mary rolled the first suitcase out into the garage and put it in the trunk of her car. She repeated the process with the remaining three. The hanging clothes she laid flat on the back seat.

She returned to the doorway one last time and looked at Adam. He was staring sadly straight ahead.

"Adam, I am so sorry," Mary told him. No response. "I don't know what happened. I don't even remember it." She watched him with pleading eyes.

Adam remained silent for only a few seconds then said almost inaudibly, "I doubt that." He still did not look at her. "You've destroyed everything."

She stared at him with pleading eyes, wishing he would look back. He did not. She nodded, turned and closed the door behind her as she left. She pulled out of the garage and reflexively pressed the button to close the garage door as she began to back out of the driveway. She turned left at the corner, drove four blocks and parked at the curb next to the park. Emotions began to overwhelm her as she began to weep.

Visions of her children came to her causing the weeping to turn into gut wrenching sobs as her stomach cramped. She could only imagine how Aric and Kara would hate her as they grew older, condemning her for what she did. She leaned in, rested her arms on the steering wheel and then laid her forehead on her arms. The weeping became a wail as she cried out, "Oh, God. Oh, God."

Chapter 3

Rhonda felt her cell phone vibrating in her scrubs pocket. She pulled it out and checked the caller ID. "Hi," she said cheerily to Mary as she answered it.

"Hi. It's me," replied Mary. Her voice told Rhonda immediately that something was wrong. "I'm in trouble. I need to talk to you."

"What's wrong?" Rhonda asked. The cheeriness left her voice.

"Adam kicked me out. I need a place to stay tonight."

"Oh my gosh," Rhonda answered as she put her palm against her cheek. "What happened?"

"I... I don't know. I need you, Rhonda. I've been hanging out here at the McDonald's because I didn't know where else to go."

"OK," Rhonda replied. "I can't get off work right now, but if you come down here to Forsythe, I can give you my key."

"OK," came Mary's whimpered reply.   Mary disconnected the call without saying goodbye.

~~~~

Forsythe Rehabilitation and Nursing Home was a ten-minute drive from the McDonald's that Mary had been camped out at for the day. It was now after dark, and the drive out of town only seemed to worsen her deepening depression. Nestled in among large trees, the parking area seemed scarily dark. There were no street lamps and no moonlight. Only a light at the building entrance gave any illumination at all. The darkness of the parking lot made her uneasy and nervous. She was acutely aware of the quiet as she walked quickly to the building entrance. The rustling of tree leaves as the wind passed through the trees was the only sound she heard.

With just steps to go, she heard a distant whistle. Her mind immediately identified it as a train whistle but she just as quickly rejected the thought. There were no trains anywhere around the area any longer. A second time the whistle blew. The sound was far away, but it seemed to resonate in her ears. It made her steps quicken even more.

As she opened the entrance door, she felt as if someone had tapped her on the back of her right shoulder. She gasped and turned only to find that no one was there. She stepped through the door and pulled it hard behind her until it closed and latched. Stepping to the side, she leaned against the floor to ceiling window next to the door and breathed hard. She did not understand what she was sensing that was frightening her. She fought to control her emotions.

Her cell phone vibrated in her front jean pocket. She instinctively reached for it and pulled it out. She looked at it, preparing to answer it and realized it was not ringing. There was no call and no messages. The distraction gave her a moment to calm herself. She had felt her phone vibrate in her pocket before when it actually had not. She would sense the vibration against her leg only to realize that it had not rung. There were times she could swear that it vibrated in her pocket when it was laying on the counter. Usually these phantom rings amused her but tonight the sensation made her more anxious.

She took a deep breath and walked down the hallway to the nursing station where she found Rhonda. As her sister looked up from her desk, Mary burst into tears. She stood with her shoulders slumped and her arms hanging down at her sides. Rhonda rushed around the counter to meet her. She wrapped her arms around Mary and held her tightly. Mary could only respond weakly and laid her head forward on Rhonda's shoulder and began to sob uncontrollably.

Rhonda held her for several seconds until Mary regained some of her composure. She signaled another nurse to take over her station and walked Mary down around the corner toward the end of the hallway.

As Rhonda opened the door to the visitor's chapel, Mary stopped. She felt that same vibration in her pocket. Hoping it was Adam calling to talk to her she pulled out her cell phone and checked it. It was another phantom ring. As she looked at the screen she heard the faint wail of a train whistle again. Mary looked blankly at her phone.

"What's wrong?" Rhonda asked her.

"What is that?" Mary asked her sister as she looked at her and cocked an ear.

"What?"

"It sounds like a train whistle."

"I didn't hear any train whistle, Mary," Rhonda told her. "Come on, let's go inside and talk."

Mary remained frozen at the door appearing to be puzzled. "Come on in," Rhonda prompted. "It's the chapel."

Mary stepped in and looked around the visitor's chapel. The dimly lit room was about half the size of a patient's room. The doorway was at the back of it on one side. A small table with a flower arrangement on top was pushed against the wall opposite of the door. The front of the chapel was adorned with a large wooden cross that angled out slightly from the top. Two small spotlights in the ceiling above it created a shadow on either side of it giving the impression of having three crosses. Beneath it, serving as an altar, was a small table covered with a simple white cloth that was neatly pressed. A padded kneeling bench ran the length of it. Three rows of five padded brown chairs filled the middle of the room. They were arranged with three chairs on one side and two on the other with a narrow aisleway running between them.

They chose seats in the last row of chairs and sat beside each other. Rhonda wrapped an arm around her sister.

"What happened?" Rhonda asked her.

Mary let her eyes go unfocused as she stared forward without answering.

"Mary, what happened?" Rhonda repeated.

"I slept with someone," Mary said flatly.

"Oh, my gosh," Rhonda reacted. "Why would you do that?" The question was reflexive and involuntary.

"I don't know. I had too much to drink and woke up this morning in bed with him."

"Who?" asked Rhonda still trying to suppress her shock.

"Gabe Fellows."

"Oh, my gosh," Rhonda repeated.

"Someone sent Adam videos of us dancing and kissing and then me leaving in his car with him."

"Oh, no," Rhonda gasped. Her eyes darted around the room wildly as her mind tried to come to grips with the details. Mary looked defeated. She sat passively as she leaned into Rhonda. "Oh, crap," Rhonda whispered.

"I didn't get home until almost ten this morning. I don't know why I did it. I was dancing, and Gabe kept bringing me drinks. I don't remember hardly any of it. I was so wasted. It was like it wasn't me in those videos Adam has."

Rhonda held her as she tried to process everything. She could only imagine how Adam would react. "What did Adam say?" she asked her.

"He screamed at me. He was so angry. I've never seen him that angry before. Then he told me to get out."

"Why wasn't Adam at the wedding?"

"Kara got sick just before we had to leave and threw up all over him."

"Oh, wow."

Rhonda continued to hold her for a few more minutes as Mary cried softly. Mary wiped her eyes and nose with a tissue. The room was quiet. Finally, Rhonda said, "I've got another hour and a half before my shift ends. I can't leave. You can stay here if you want or I can give you my key and meet you at my apartment."

The thought of being alone in Rhonda's apartment seemed overwhelming. "Can I stay here and wait for you?" she asked.

"Yes. Of course. I'll be either just outside or down the hall if you need me."

"Thanks," Mary told her as Rhonda stood to leave.

Rhonda stopped to look at her. "You'll get through this," she told Mary. "Everything will be alright. I promise." Mary nodded. Rhonda left the room.

Ralph Nelson Willett

Chapter 4

It was less than an hour before Mary felt strong enough to go to Rhonda's apartment and wait for her. She had knelt on the kneeling bench and prayed. Her prayers felt weak and useless. It had been so long since she had prayed and now when she needed to, she felt as if God no longer heard her. But she did feel better. She decided she could leave and wait for Rhonda at her apartment.

"Mary?" A voice from a dark room across the hall beckoned her just as she stepped out of the chapel. She froze in her tracks and tried to see into the darkness of the room across the hall. She was not sure if the voice was calling her name or not.

"Mary?" the voice called again. "Would you step in here please?"

Mary tilted her head as she tried to focus her eyes into the darkness. She wondered who was in there that knew her. She stepped cautiously forward to the door. As she approached, she could see the form of someone sitting in a chair on the far side of the room. "Are you calling me?" she asked.

"I've heard the whistles," the voice said. The shakiness of the voice let Mary know it was an older gentleman speaking.

"Are you talking to me?" Mary asked again.

"If your name is Mary, then yesss." The 'yes' seemed to be exaggerated in both how deep and low the tone of it was, but also how long he dragged it out. It ended with a long hissing sound.

Mary realized she was leaning into the room hunched over and straightened herself. "What whistles?"

"I heard you talking to the nurse. I've heard the train whistles many times. Yesss."

"You have?" asked Mary. "I don't think she believed me."

"Please," the old man said. "Come in for just a moment. You can turn on the light."

Mary did not want to talk with anyone. Every fiber of her body objected. She did not feel up to any personal interaction, especially someone she did not know, especially not now, not today.

"Please," the old man said again. "This will only take a moment."

Mary closed her eyes, and her shoulders slumped as she felt herself surrender to the request. She stepped further into the room and turned the light on. On the far side of the room, she saw an old man sitting in a winged back chair. His eyes were clouded bright white. A red blanket lay over his lap with a white cane lying across his legs.

"Hello, Mary," he said holding a shaking hand to her. "My name is Aluishous Gregory Blunt, but please, just call me Allie."

Mary took his hand. It felt fragile. It felt as if she squeezed, even the slightest, his hand would be crushed within her grip. She shook it gently. "Hi, Allie. I'm pleased to meet you." She heard the weariness in her own voice.

"Yesss, I've heard the whistles many times," he told her. "Two short and one long." Mary noted again that when he said 'yes' it was drawn out, starting at a higher pitch and then dropping to a low pitch that seemed to come from the depths of his chest.

"That's what I heard," Mary responded. "Two short and one long."

"Yesss." Again the 'yes' was drawn out, starting with a higher tone sliding down to a low rumble. "There's a sad story behind that whistle. Yesss. Would you like to hear it?"

Mary did not think she could handle a sad story at the moment. Her own story felt so overwhelmingly sad that she was already feeling as if depression were crashing in on her like an ocean wave. She did not want to accelerate it with a sad story. "I don't know if I can handle anything more that's sad today."

"Yesss. I can hear the sadness in your voice." He reached out with his cane and tapped a nearby chair. "Sit for a moment. We can talk."

"I'm sorry," Mary told him. "I really need to get going."

"Yesss," he replied again drawing it out.

"But thanks for letting me know at least someone else has heard the whistles." She turned to leave the room. "I have to leave. Good night."

"Have you noticed that there aren't any trains here anymore?" he asked. Mary froze. "There are no train tracks here any longer."

Mary turned to face him again. Her mind raced trying to process what he just said. "I know," she replied quietly. "So, it can't be a train whistle."

Allie tapped the empty chair again. "Yesss. It is a train; a steam locomotive."

Mary stood a moment staring at the old man. His white hair needed to be trimmed, and it seemed his ears were too big for his head. He looked straight ahead with blind eyes as he rested the tip of the white cane on the empty chair. Allie removed the cane when Mary moved hesitantly toward the chair. She sat on its edge as if she was prepared to run at any moment. "OK," she began. "How can it be a train?"

"To understand the whistles then you need to know the story. It is sad. Yesss."

"OK, I'm curious. Is it a long story?"

"It's a short story, but like many things, it will last forever," he told her.

Mary smiled weakly at him. It occurred to her that he just needed a bit of company. Many seniors here had no visitors at all. She decided she could use the distraction. It delayed her having to go to Rhonda's empty apartment. "It's short but it will last forever," she repeated. "What does that mean?"

"Yesss," he said. "Let me tell you what it is, how it was told to me. The Great War had ended, and all the soldiers were coming home. Many men died and never returned. Do you know what the Great War was?"

"That was World War Two," she answered.

"No, it was not." He drew out his 'no' in the same manner he did with his 'yes.' Its tone was deep. "It was World War One."

"I'm sorry. I never was good at history."

"Yes," he replied. He did not say more. Just as Mary was beginning to think he was not going to continue, he began again. "Before the war, a very young Charles Moore took a job in the city. He had just been married, and he was doing his best to take care of his new bride, but he could only find work in the city. But he and his bride chose to live here, right in our own town. Every Monday he would ride the train into the city, and every Friday night he would return to be with his beautiful wife. They knew that someday they would no longer have to live that way.

"Everyone liked Charles. He had a smile that went on forever, kind of like this story." He paused just long enough to face Mary and grin at her as if he had just told a joke. He continued. "Well, the engineer liked Charles also, and he would let him ride in the cab with them on Friday nights. Just outside of town, Charles would blow the train whistle to let his bride know he was close; two short and one long, always two short and one long."

Allie stopped telling the story and sat quietly. Mary waited, thinking there was more but Allie did not continue. "So, what happened?" Mary asked.

"Yesss," Allie said. "The war came. Everyone wanted to join the army and fight the Huns. Everyone thought they would be a hero. No one ever thought that they would die there and never see home again. War is like that. Young men do not believe they will die. So many men did not come back from that war, so many men."

He reached over with his cane and tapped her leg lightly. "Too many men died, Mary. Yesss."

Allie paused. Mary prompted him again, "I know. We should never have war."

"Yesss. But we did have war, and we still do. Yesss. People killing people has been a way of life since Cain killed Abel. Man has turned killing into an art because men like to kill men. Yesss."

"So, was Charles killed in the war?" Mary prompted.

"No. He was not. He survived. Not even a scratch. His ship landed in New York, and he was returning with other men that survived from our town. Yesss. They boarded the train in the city. It was a Friday night, the Friday night they came home. Yesss. Home. Yesss." Allie paused for a moment to gather his thoughts then continued, "That same engineer was in the same cab of the same engine of that very same train that the young husband used to ride on the way home to his bride. Yesss, he was. That engineer saw Charles and invited him to ride once more with him in the cab of the locomotive. Of course, Charles accepted. Yesss. As they came close to town..." He stopped and turned his head to face her. "Do you know where the old railroad bridge is that crosses the river? I have heard that they turned it into a covered foot bridge now. Yesss."

"Yeah, I know it," Mary answered. "I know where it's at."

"Yes. It is a trail now. It was once train tracks. Now it is a trail. Yesss." He faced forward again as Mary waited for him to continue. "Just before the bridge is where Charles would blow the whistle, two short and one long, always two short and one long, to let his bride know he was coming. Three times he blew the whistle. Three times. Yesss." He waited a moment again. "His wife heard that whistle. She did. Yesss. She heard his whistle. Until that very moment, she did not know when he would be coming home. Until that very moment, she did not know if he had survived the war. The letters he had sent her after the war ended somehow did not arrive until many weeks later." He stopped talking again. After a moment, he hummed one long note that seemed to rattle in his chest, "Hummmmmmmmmm. The Great War. Nothing great about war. Yesss." He faced her again and tapped her leg lightly again with his cane. "Are you still here, Mary?"

"Yes, sir. I'm still here."

"Yesss," he said, drawing it out again and ending it with a long hiss of the 's'. "Two short and one long. His bride heard the whistle and knew he was alive and nearly home in her arms again. She ran to meet him at the station. But he never arrived, Mary."

He stopped until Mary prodded him again, "What happened?"

"Just before the train reached the bridge, a tree fell on the tracks in front of them. It was not a big tree. It was a small tree, but Charles was leaning out of the window blowing the whistle. A branch from that tree pierced through his throat. It killed him just minutes from the embrace of his beautiful bride."

Mary looked at him as an anger boiled deep inside her. She was clenching her jaw and stared at his face. He turned slowly and faced her. His blind, blank eyes seemed to be looking into hers.

"I said it was a sad story," Allie told her. "Yesss."

"So, you're trying to tell me that a ghost is making the train whistle?" she asked incredulously.

"Ghost?" Allie asked. "I did not say anything about a ghost, but that is the story. Yesss."

Mary stood. "I don't think so," she said. "Anyhow, I have to be going now."

"So, Mary," he said as he tapped her leg again with his cane. "Does every story end happily ever after?"

"What?"

"Yesss," he said. "I hear the anger in your voice. You are angry because you believe I told you a ghost story. But tell me this; I hear the same whistles you hear. Just me. Just you. We hear them. Are there ghosts in our lives calling out to us?"

"I have to go, Mr. Blunt."

"Yesss."

Mary turned and left the room flicking off the light as she left. She walked quickly down to the nurse's station where she found Rhonda was just preparing to end her shift. "Just in time," Rhonda told her.

"I'll meet you at your apartment," Mary said wearily. She let herself out and stepped into the cool November night air. She did not understand why she felt angry with the old man. She had heard ghost stories before and was never bothered by any of them. What was different about this one? Was she bothered by the story or was she bothered that she let an old man waste her time?

She unlocked the car with her key fob from where she stood at the building entrance. The locks made a thumping sound, and the car's lights lit up. She used the car lights to guide her through the dark parking lot. As she approached the car and put her hand on the door handle, she stopped to listen. She could hear the wind blowing through the trees. There was nothing else. Train whistles, she thought. Why am I listening for train whistles?

Chapter 5

Rhonda helped Mary bring her suitcases down into her lower level apartment and set them down just inside the door. Mary looked around the apartment from the doorway. She had been in her sister's apartment many times, but tonight everything felt different.

"Want anything to eat?" Rhonda asked her.

"No thank you."

"Something to drink?"

"No thank you." Mary stepped inside and closed the door behind her. She felt as if her life had boiled down to just these four suitcases. She felt as if everything else had been stripped from her. "Can I sleep on your couch?" she asked.

"Yes, of course."

Mary shed her jacket and placed it on the back of a kitchen chair. She walked over and sat on the sofa and stared at the floor. Rhonda sat down beside her.

"You must have had a lot to drink," Rhonda told her. "That's not like you."

A moment had passed before Mary answered. "But that's what I did."

"Did Gabe say anything?"

"No. I left too quickly after I woke up in bed with him. I was too sick to my stomach."

Rhonda reached over and held her sister's hand with both of hers. It was cold and trembling. "Do you think Adam will calm down?" Rhonda asked her.

Mary shook her head almost imperceptibly. "I've never seen him that mad before. He's never screamed at me like that before."

"I know when Nick and I broke up I was doing all the screaming," Rhonda told her quietly. "But he was the one that cheated."

Mary looked away from Rhonda with a pained look. "You're not helping," she told her.

"I'm sorry," Rhonda answered. "I didn't mean it that way. What I meant was I understand the screaming because that's what I did when Nick and I broke up."

They sat quietly there for several moments when Mary spoke up. "There's a difference. Nick made a choice to cheat. I don't even remember doing it."

"You can go see Adam in the morning, or call him," Rhonda told her. "Maybe by then, he'll calm down enough to talk."

"I hope so." Mary looked her sister in the face. Tears were welling up again in Mary's eyes and were starting to run down her cheeks. "I," she said just before her throat choked off the word. She struggled to force the words out and wiped her eyes. She tried again. "I don't want to lose him." Her lip trembled before the next sentence gushed out a wail. "I don't want to lose Adam."

Rhonda wrapped her arms around Mary and held her tightly as she sobbed. "Oh God, I'm so sorry, Mary," she repeated.

~~~~

Sunday morning Mary awoke to the smell of coffee and sat up on the sofa.

"Good morning," Rhonda said from the kitchen table trying to add a brightness to her voice.

"Good morning," Mary replied quietly.

"You want something to eat?"

Mary took a quick inventory of how she felt. She was stiff and perhaps a little sore from sleeping on the sofa, but she was not hungry. "No thank you," she replied. "What time is it?"

"Almost nine thirty."

Mary brushed her hair back with both hands and then ran her hands over her face. "I guess I could use some coffee, though."

"Got it," Rhonda said as she stood from her chair. "Black? Cream?"

"A little milk please," Mary said as she stood and stretched her back. She walked over to the kitchen table just as Rhonda handed her a coffee mug. "Thank you," Mary told her.

Mary pulled out a chair from the opposite side of the table from Rhonda, and they both sat down.

"So, what are your plans for today?" Rhonda asked her.

"I'm going to try and go see Adam again."

"You think he'll talk to you?"

"I don't know," Mary answered. "This is all new territory for me. I don't know what to expect."

"He's had a chance to sleep on it. I'm sure he'll at least talk to you."

"I hope so. I want to fix this."

They sat without speaking for a while as they both sipped their coffee. Rhonda finally broke the silence. "Was anything going on between you two before this happened?"

Mary looked at her inquisitively. "What do you mean?"

"I mean were you having some trouble before? Is this the first time anything like this has happened?"

Mary swore in frustration. "No. How could you even ask that? I've never even looked at another guy before."

"What about him?"

Mary tilted her head as she considered it. "No. I don't think so. Why?"

"I'm just thinking," Rhonda told her. "I'm no shrink, but if he was cheating, then he may overreact to cover up his own feelings of guilt."

Mary stared into her coffee and began to speak slowly. "I don't think so. I screwed up. I think if he did what I did I'd be mad too. Do you think he's overreacting?"

"I don't know," Rhonda answered as she appeared to think through the question. "Maybe." A moment had passed before Rhonda redirected the question. "Do you think he'll be vindictive?"

"I don't know," she answered after a moment. "I don't know what I'd do if it was me. I can't see Adam cheating."

"But you can see yourself cheating?" Rhonda asked her.

"No, I can't. I don't know how it came to this. All I wanted to do was dance." Mary's eyes were beginning to tear again, but she held the tears back.

Rhonda decided to back away from the subject. "OK, is there anything you need?"

"No. I think I'm just going to get dressed and go home and see if I can talk to him."

~~~

Mary spent the next hour showering, applying makeup and dressing. As she pulled into the driveway, she pressed the garage door opener. It did not open. Panic rushed through her as the thought came to her that Adam may have changed the code to the garage door opener. Then the thought occurred to her that Adam may have changed all the locks. Her breathing became short and shallow as she parked the car in front of the garage door and climbed out. Walking around to the side door, her hand trembled as she put the key in the lock. It did not open the door. She pulled it out and tried again, wiggling it hard. Still, the lock remained firm. Adam had changed the locks.

She rang the doorbell and waited. No answer. Again, she rang the doorbell and again no answer. The feeling of panic deepened. She walked quickly, nearly jogging to the front door. Again, she tried her key, and again the lock did not budge. In resignation, she sat on the landing of the front steps, wrapped her arms around herself and stared down at the sidewalk. Intellectually she knew Adam probably took the children to church but emotionally she felt that he should be here. He should be home.

Thoughts of separation and divorce raced painfully through her mind. She wondered where she would go and what she would do. Conversations with Adam played out in her head. She envisioned herself apologizing to him and Adam expressing his anger. She could hear Adam sharing how badly hurt he was. Mary would apologize repeatedly, and ultimately the conversation would end in an embrace. They could get counseling. They could get through this. She would do whatever it took to make amends.

But one scenario continued to force its way to the forefront of her mind. It haunted her. It was the one where he said he was through and wanted a divorce. Mary's stomach churned at the thought. What would this mean for her? She thought about being alone. She already felt alone. She felt abandoned. The one person she could always depend on to be there for her had just locked her out of her house.

She pulled her coat tight to ward off the cold weather and looked around the neighborhood. She realized that she did not know any of her neighbors well, but suddenly she felt she was going to miss them. Unless she could be reconciled to Adam, she could no longer live in this house, in this neighborhood with these neighbors. It was hard to think about, but she wondered if she would ever live in such a nice house again. She wondered if she would ever again live in such a quiet neighborhood with its manicured lawns and curving streets.

She heard a car pulling into the driveway and looked up to see Adam pulling in. He stopped the car, backed up and then parked in the street in front of the house. The kids waved at her from the back seat. Aric climbed out and ran up to his Mother as Adam let Kara out of her car seat.

"Hi, Mom," Aric greeted. "We stayed at Grandma's house."

Mary put on a smile for him. "That's good. Did you have a good time?"

"Yeah. I helped Grandma make cookies and then Grandpa and me went fishing at the lake."

"Fishing? Wow. Did you get anything?"

"Yep. I caught two bluegills. But I had to throw them back because they were too small. How come we didn't go to church today?"

Mary turned to see Kara running up to her with Adam walking slowly behind her. Kara held out her arms for

Mary to pick her up. "Hi, sweetie." Mary told her as she gave Kara a kiss on the cheek."

"We stayed at Grandma's house," Kara told her, repeating what Aric had just said.

"I heard that," Mary said, trying to show some excitement. "Did you have fun?"

"Yes. I made cookies."

"Did you bring me some?"

"No. They're at Grandma's house," Kara told her with a hint of disappointment in her voice.

Aric stood directly in front of Mary. "Why didn't we go to church today?" he asked again.

Mary looked up at Adam as he approached them. "Well," she began as she tried to come up with a suitable explanation. "I think that Mommy and Daddy just needed a break for today. We'll go next week."

Adam stood off to the side as he watched Mary and the children interact. Mary looked over at him. He still looked angry. "Why don't you two go in the house so Mommy and I can talk for a minute?" he asked the kids. He stepped past Mary, unlocked the front door and let the kids inside. Aric and Kara bounced into the house. Mary stood and stepped down to the sidewalk.

Adam turned to Mary from the landing and looked down at her. He appeared even angrier. "What do you need, Mary?"

"You changed the locks," Mary stated.

"Yes. You don't live here anymore," Adam said as he came down the steps to face her. His body seemed to brace for the inevitable fight.

"Adam, can we talk about this?"

"I've got nothing more to say," he responded.

"Adam, I am so sorry. He doesn't mean anything to me. It was an accident. Please forgive me."

"I don't care. I can never forgive you for this." He leaned in toward her. "I will *never* forgive you for this," he said through clenched teeth.

Mary flinched at his aggressive posture. She reached out a hand toward his arm to touch it. He pulled it back. "Please Adam," Mary begged. "I don't want to lose you. I love you."

"Yeah," Adam replied tersely.

"I am so sorry. I'll do whatever I need to do to make it up to you. Please forgive me."

"No. This has been coming for a long time. You finally forced me to do something. It's over." His voice was calm and measured as he struggled to keep his anger in check.

Mary looked confused. "What do you mean it's been coming for a long time."

Adam was shaking. "It's been a long time since you felt any physical attraction to me. I thought I could work it out, *we* could work it out, but then I saw you with *him*. That's when I realized that it was over."

"What do you mean I haven't felt any physical attraction to you? That's not true. Yes, I have." Mary was beginning to speak more quickly.

Adam's trembling became more pronounced. "Really? Really?" He took one short step toward her. "When was the last time we made love?"

Mary thought for a moment but could not remember the last time.

"Yeah," he said drawing out the word. "I remember. It's been over two months."

"Adam, I'm sorry."

"You know, I've been thinking about this, and it keeps running through my mind over and over again," he said. "Friday, when you were checking out your bridesmaid dress, I started kissing your neck, what did you tell me?"

Mary could not remember.

"You said 'it's going to be a long day so don't get your hopes up.' Then I see you all over that guy. You certainly didn't look tired to me. Did you think I wouldn't be hurt? Did you think I wouldn't be mad?" He took another short step toward her. He leaned in toward her, squinted his eyes and with a quiet, measured voice said, "Did you think it wouldn't be over?"

Mary nearly gasped as she took one step back away from Adam. "Adam, I am so sorry. You could have told me how you were feeling. I didn't know. We can fix this. We can get counseling."

"What makes you think I'm interested in fixing it now?" he asked as he relaxed his posture.

"Please, Adam. I can do better."

Adam huffed at her. "You can do better..." he sneered. "I've seen your better. You've saved your better for someone else."

"I don't know what happened Friday night. I can't remember. That's not like me at all. But I do know that I love you and don't want to lose you. I'm sorry that I haven't been as affectionate as I should be but with work and the kids, I'm just tired."

Adam's trembling stopped. The darkness that his spirit felt and showed on his face seemed to fade. "Mary," he began calmly. "We're done. I can't do this anymore." His voice was now almost casual.

Mary's eyes began to tear. "What can I do?" she asked him quietly. "I'll do anything to keep us together."

"It's over, Mary," he replied. "You've done enough."

Mary's tears began to run slowly down her face. "What are you going to do?"

Adam looked at her almost compassionately. "I'm going to file. We'll share custody of the kids. I'm not interested in trying to take them from you as long as you don't create a problem."

Mary wiped her face. "I don't know what I'm going to do," she told him softly.

"You'll figure it out."

Mary stood in front of him for a moment as she thought. Finally, she spoke as her voice was nearly choked off. "I'm so sorry. I ruined everything."

"Yes, you did," he replied calmly.

"I'll need to come back and get some more of my things."

"Call me when you're ready. I'll come home and let you in."

"Can I say good-bye to the kids?"

"Of course."

Mary walked up the steps and placed her hand on the door handle. She hesitated before opening the door. The house suddenly felt foreign to her. It did not feel like home any longer. The handle felt hot in her hand, and she could feel herself trembling. She turned to look down at Adam who was watching her from below. He seemed almost peaceful. Mary opened the door and went in.

She walked the hall slowly to the living room and peeked in just as she turned the corner. Aric and Kara were both parked on the floor in front of the TV watching a cartoon.

"Kids," she began. Her voice was weak.

"Hi, Mom," replied Aric without turning away from the TV to look at her.

Kara turned around and saw her mother behind her. She stood and walked over to her. She looked worried. She held both arms up to her mother. Mary leaned over and took one of her hands and hugged Kara against her legs. "Why are you crying, Mommy?" Kara asked.

Aric turned around quickly and at seeing his mother crying, leaped up and rushed over to her. "What's wrong?" he asked.

Mary squatted in front of them and pulled them both to her as she hugged them. She opened her mouth to speak, but no words came.

Kara began to cry involuntarily, not understanding why her mother was crying.

"What's wrong?" Aric asked again on the verge of crying himself.

Again, Mary tried to speak, and again no words came out. She trembled as she held her children. Kara was now crying loudly, and Aric began to cry. After several moments, Mary told them, "I have to go."

"Where you going?" Aric whimpered over Kara's crying.

"I have to go stay with your Aunt Rhonda for a while. Daddy and I need to fix a couple of things then I'll be back, OK?"

"No," Aric replied.

"I'm sorry, Sweetie," she told him. "I have to. We'll get together a lot, I promise."

Kara began to cry louder. Mary hugged them tightly and then wiped her face again.

"Can I come with you?" Aric asked through his own crying.

"No. I'm sorry. Not this time. I just need to be with your Aunt Rhonda for a while. You'll be fine here with Daddy."

Aric stepped back leaving room for Kara to rush in tightly to both of Mary's arms. She cried loudly, only understanding that her mother was upset. Mary picked her up and stood. She turned to see Adam watching dispassionately from the hall. She walked slowly to him, gave Kara another tight hug and then handed her over to Adam who held her with one arm. She turned to face Aric one last time who stood with his arms hanging at his sides, his head bowed and crying. "I'll see you later, Honey," she said to him. She then leaned in and gave Kara a kiss on the cheek. Kara held her arms out to her again, but Mary stepped back away from her. She took one last moment to look at her children who were both sobbing uncontrollably. She then looked at Adam. Adam's face had softened with the crying of his children. His eyes reflected sadness. Mary made an abrupt turn away and walked quickly back out the front door. She climbed in her car and backed out of the driveway. Just as she began pulling away, she looked to see Adam and the children standing in the doorway watching her leave.

Chapter 6

Mary and Rhonda sat at Rhonda's kitchen table as they discussed what would be needed for the new apartment. Rhonda was reviewing the list she had made in the spiral notebook when a knock came at the door. Mary exchanged glances with her as Rhonda stood to answer it.

Rhonda looked through the peep hole then turned and whispered loudly to Mary, "It's your pastor."

"Let him in," Mary said smiling as she stood and began moving toward the door.

Rhonda opened the door. Pastor David Flynn was a tall man, perhaps six foot four. In his mid-fifties, he still had an athletic build. He wore black slacks, a blue striped collared shirt and black shoes that were polished to almost a mirror finish. "Hi, I'm Pastor Flynn. I'd like to speak with Mary," he said as he nodded toward her."

"Sure," Rhonda replied as she moved from the doorway to allow him in.

"Hi, Pastor," Mary said as she greeted him at the door.

"Hi, Mary. Can we talk for a minute?"

"Yes," Mary replied pleasantly. "Let's sit over here," she directing him toward the sofa. Mary was genuinely pleased to see him. His presence gave her the first glimmer of hope she has had through all of this. She guided him toward the sofa. He chose to sit in the glider rocker next to it and rested his elbows on his knees as he leaned in toward her. She sat on the edge of the sofa and faced him.

Immediately Mary began to feel an unease. Pastor Flynn did not appear to be pleased to be here. Her smile began to fade quickly.

"Mary," he began, "we take adultery very seriously. This is the part of my job that I like the least. I don't like having to confront sin like this."

Mary's heart sank. Her entire body began to slump. She was beginning to feel the need to run.

"But I have to ask you, Mary, did you do it?" he looked at her compassionately.

Mary could not respond. She was stunned, and at a loss for words. She tried to speak, but no words came out. She finally gave up and looked down at the floor.

Flynn nodded but did not take his eyes off her. "As I said, this is the part of my job I like the least. Mary, I need to ask you not to return to church. Perhaps in a few months, after things have settled down between you and Adam and you've demonstrated your repentance, then we can talk again."

Mary looked up at him in disbelief. Her jaw dropped. "You're kicking me out?" she asked.

Flynn nodded again. "Mary, we can't let it appear that we tolerate adultery within our church. It's too serious of a thing. I have to ask you not to return."

From across the room, Rhonda jumped out of the kitchen chair she was sitting in, nearly knocking it over. She swore loudly and angrily at him. "You have got to be kidding!" she shouted at him. "You're kicking her out? Just when she needs you the most you're gonna throw her out of the church?"

Flynn looked at Rhonda angrily. "You don't need to use that kind of language," he said.

Rhonda swore at him again. "You're in my house! I live here! You don't! I'll use any language I want to use!" She began walking toward him pointing her finger at him like a gun. "I always knew you people were hypocrites! Talking about how you love your neighbor and all that crap!"

Flynn stood to meet Rhonda. She stood in front of him and poked her finger in his chest as she looked up into his face. "Just when she needs a church, you kick her out! I want you out of my apartment, now!"

Flynn looked down on her in shock. He had not expected to be challenged in this manner. "Look, I don't like this..." he began.

Rhonda interrupted him by shouting louder and pointing at the door. "Now!" she shouted.

Flynn blinked a couple of times and then stepped sideways to step around Rhonda. Rhonda rotated around watching Flynn as he walked quickly to the door. He placed a hand on the handle and then turned back to face Mary. "I'm sorry, Mary," he said. "I'm sorry I have to do this." Rhonda turned around and took a magazine from the end table and threw it hard at him. Its pages opened and fluttered as it flew toward him. It had lost most of its energy before it hit the wall beside him. Flynn quickly opened the door, stepped through and closed it behind him.

Rhonda stared at the door angrily with pursed lips. She clenched her fists at her sides as she breathed heavily, shoulders rising and falling with each breath. After a moment, she turned to look down at Mary sitting on the sofa. She had put her feet up on the cushion and was hugging her knees to her chest. She rested her chin on her knees as she stared straight forward.

"That's why I don't go to church," Rhonda said, as she stretched her arm out with a finger pointing at the door. Mary acted as if she had not heard her. Rhonda calmed herself and sat down next to Mary and wrapped an arm around her. "Are you OK?" she asked in a soothing voice.

"Yeah," Mary responded unconvincingly.

"You can forget those people. There's nothing there for you."

"I know."

Rhonda gave her a squeeze. "Is there anything I can do for you?" she asked her.

"No," Mary responded while not looking at her. "I really just want to be left alone." Mary's voice sounded sleepy. "What difference does any of it make now?" she asked.

Ralph Nelson Willett

Chapter 7

Mary slouched in her chair behind her desk at the head of her classroom. The room was empty now, and the halls were quiet. The stack of papers seemed daunting even though it was smaller than usual. Of her six classes needing review, she had worked her way through only one. She thought about taking the papers back to Rhonda's apartment and finishing there, but Rhonda would be away at work. Just thinking about spending another night alone fed her depression. It was better just to work from her classroom desk. This was one of those days she wished she had a student teacher to assist her. She could hand off the mundane work to her, but as she thought about it, she decided that the mundane and routine task kept her sane.

It had been two weeks since the wedding. What little she could remember played out in her mind over and over. She could remember drinking her first beer and wanting to dance. Everything else from that night was lost in the black out. She had given up trying to remember anything more.

A knock came at her door, and Miranda Baraga peeked her head in. "Can I come in?" she asked.

Mary gave her a smile and a nod. "Yeah. Come on in," she told her as she sat up straighter in her chair. Miranda was a new teacher in the school this year. Mary did not know her well but knew she had followed her husband to the area when he took a new job just outside of River Run.

Miranda stepped in and sat in a chair beside her desk. "I just thought I'd stop in and see how you're doing," she told Mary.

"I'm fine," Mary told her. "I just can't get motivated to go through these papers."

They were silent for a moment. Miranda smiled kindly at her. "Mary," Miranda said, "I know it's none of my business and I hope you won't mind me asking, but I'd like to know if you're really doing OK."

Mary looked at her blankly. "I'm OK, I guess," Mary said.

"I know you had some trouble with your husband. I can understand how hard that might be."

Anger flared in Mary. Was she angry? Was she angry that this woman she hardly knew would want to pry into her private life? The emotion passed quickly as she saw the kindness in Miranda's face. Mary only nodded.

"Is there anything I can do to help?" Miranda asked.

"No, but thanks for asking," Mary responded. "How'd you hear?"

"The rumor mill has kicked in. I try not to tune into it, but there are times when I'd like to see if I can help. Like I said, it's really none of my business, and it's OK to tell me so."

"You're fine," Mary told her. "I'm sure everybody knows by now anyhow."

"Can I take you out for some coffee or maybe buy you some dinner?" Miranda asked. "My husband is working late tonight, and I could use some company. I'll buy."

Mary thought about it for a moment. She could use some company, someone to talk to. The thought of going back to Rhonda's apartment just seemed too depressing. She accepted.

~~~

Mary had never been to the little restaurant that Miranda suggested although she had driven by it many times. It was small with only a few tables and a row of five booths on one wall. The waitress was young, perhaps in her late teens. The tips of her hair were tinted blue with pink stripes going down the sides. Several colorful tattoos adorned her arms. She wore large hooped earrings, and one ear was adorned with several piercings running up its edge.

"Hi, Miranda," the waitress said cheerily as she set glasses of water in front of them. "Welcome back."

"Thanks, Kelly. This is my friend, Mary," Miranda said as she pointed to Mary. "Mary, this is Kelly. Her dad owns this restaurant."

Mary nodded to Kelly.

Kelly handed a menu to each of them. "Is there anything I can get you now?" she asked.

"Give us a few," Miranda said.

"Sure," Kelly said. "I'll let Dad know you're here."

"Thanks," Miranda replied.

Mary watched as Kelly walked back into the kitchen. "You must come here a lot," she said to Miranda.

"A couple of times a month, maybe," Miranda replied. "The food's pretty good. Her dad used to be a cook in the Navy. When he retired, he bought this place. His wife and daughter help him with it."

Mary grinned at her. "You seem to know a lot about them for only coming here a couple of times a month."

Miranda smiled back. "We attend the same church together. When we first moved here, we were in the same small group. My husband was in the Navy just after high school. He and Don swap stories all the time. They're really good people."

"Church," Mary said coldly. "I can't go back to my church."

Miranda squinted at her. "Why not?"

"Because it would be too awkward. Adam still goes there and takes the kids. With everything that happened I don't think I could take it." Mary looked down, paused for a moment then added, "I don't think they want me going back there."

Mary looked back up to see compassion in Miranda's eyes. "I'm sorry," Miranda said. "I know it's hard."

"Yeah," Mary said. She felt a wave of guilt come over her and she bit her lip. "Miranda," Mary said. "do you know what happened."

"Not really," Miranda said. "I try not to tune into the rumor mill. I think if you wanted me to know then you'd tell me."

"I cheated on my husband," Mary said guiltily. "He threw me out." Mary looked for the judgment in Miranda's eyes but did not see it. She did not know why she felt the urge to tell Miranda the details of her life, but somehow it felt right. "I didn't mean to," she added. "I got drunk. I didn't intend on even drinking that night. I drank myself into a black out, and I can't remember anything. I just woke up in bed with a guy the next morning."

"And your husband threw you out," Miranda stated mater of factly as she nodded and looked down at the table. She looked up again at Mary and asked, "Is there anything you need? Anything I can do to help?"

Mary shook her head. "Thank you, but no. I don't think so," she said. "I'm staying with my sister until I can get my own place."

"Have you tried talking to your minister at all?" Miranda asked.

"Yeah," Mary answered with a sneer. "He told me not to come back to church again. He didn't want someone like me going to his church."

Miranda was dumbfounded. "Someone like what?"

"An adulterer. He said I could come back after I straightened my life around."

"You're kidding, right?" Miranda said, unable to contain her disbelief.

Mary shook her head. "He said I had to demonstrate some kind of repentance. I don't even know what that means." Mary looked into Miranda's face. Miranda looked as if she could feel Mary's pain.

"I'm so sorry, Mary," Miranda told her. "What church is that?"

"I don't want to think about them anymore," Mary said as she shook her head. "I am so done with church." She pursed her lips and added, "Or with God for that matter."

"Oh, Mary," Miranda said as she reached across the table to touch her arm. "Please don't blame God for that. That was just some guy screwing up. Churches are for people that need help. Even Jesus said that healthy people don't need doctors. Only the sick do. Where else are you supposed to go if you can't go to your own church?"

Mary shook her head slowly and looked away. "I don't think I need church," she said.

Miranda could feel her pain. "Mary, please don't give up on God," she said. She looked out of the restaurant window a moment. When she turned back she added, "or on church. Why don't you come with me this Sunday? We'd love to have you. Then maybe Don and I can take you out to lunch."

Mary thought about it for a moment and considered her choices. She could stay in Rhonda's apartment, or she could go out and do something. Miranda was being a friend at a time when she was losing friends. "OK," she said in resignation. She never thought to ask what church it was.

Ralph Nelson Willett

Chapter 8

"Well, I guess it's home," Mary said to Rhonda as they looked over Mary's new apartment. Mary had lived with Rhonda for three weeks, sleeping on the sofa until this apartment became available. It was sparse. She took the sofa from the rec room at the house along with the TV and TV stand. She had purchased a small table and chair set for her kitchen and a bed for herself. The two twin beds for the room that Kara and Aric would use when they stayed with her would be delivered in a few days. Most of her belongings were still in boxes and plastic totes scattered around the rooms.

Mary had been relieved when Adam did not give her a hard time about the items she wanted from the house. She had expected a fight and braced herself for it, but Adam did not object when she told him over the phone what she wanted.

Miranda volunteered her husband Don and his pickup truck to help her move. When she arrived at the house to pick up her things, Kara and Aric were at their grandparent's house. Adam sat waiting for her in a chair on the front porch. Mary had greeted him, but he said nothing back. He only turned his head toward her and stared at her through nearly opaque sunglasses. Mary could see the tautness in his face as he clenched his teeth. She walked past him, leading her new friends into the house. She took the furniture they had agreed she would take. Adam had packed several boxes that waited for her. They carried them to the back of the truck. Their entire time there lasted less than thirty minutes. Adam remained in the chair on the porch without speaking a word to anyone. He only stood when the three of them climbed in the truck to leave. He leaned against a porch pillar with his arms crossed to watch as the truck backed out of the driveway. Mary took one last look at Adam as they drove away. He rotated his head to follow them as they drove past, his lips curled in an angry sneer.

Her apartment was in the same complex as Rhonda's. Behind it was the playground that the kids could use, something the house did not have. Mary and Adam had agreed that the kids would alternate staying with Adam a week and then with Mary. She was grateful that Adam was not going to fight her for shared custody of the children. Beginning next week, they would start staying with her in the apartment every other week.

"It won't take long to settle in," Rhonda told her as they both sat on the sofa.

"I know," Mary said. "I don't have much to put away. I don't have much of anything anymore. I've been married ten years, and my life boils down to just this." She swept her arm in front of her across the room.

Rhonda remained quiet for a moment. She reached behind her head and released the pony tail she wore. "It's more than I had when I got divorced," Rhonda told her. "Nick fought me for everything right down to the last spoon."

"It's a good thing you didn't have kids," Mary said.

Rhonda turned to face her. "I wanted kids," she told Mary. "I still do. I still envy you because you have kids. Nick and I tried but now all I've got from six years of being married are the scars he left me with when he cheated." Rhonda heard the words coming out of her own mouth, and instantly regretted using the word "cheated." Mary winced almost imperceptibly, but Rhonda saw the pain in her eyes. "I'm sorry," Rhonda said trying to recover. "It was different when Nick cheated. He was stone cold sober and knew exactly what he was doing. You don't even remember doing it. I'm not even sure that should be considered cheating."

Mary looked down at the floor. "So, you think that just because I was drunk that it wasn't cheating? Adam obviously doesn't think so." She turned to look out of the ground floor window. "And neither would I," she added softly.

Mary suddenly snapped her head to face Rhonda. She put on a big smile and pointed her finger at the window.

"There!" she said. "Hear that? I know you heard that one."

"What?" Rhonda asked as she looked to where Mary was pointing.

"The train whistle!" Mary said.

"I didn't hear anything."

"Then you need your hearing checked," Mary said. "Two short whistles and one long. I told you I wasn't dreaming it."

Rhonda looked back at Mary with a puzzled look. "I didn't hear anything."

"I'm not crazy," Mary protested. "I hear a train. It's even louder now. How can you *not* hear that?"

Rhonda squinted and tilted her head as she looked back at Mary.

"Oh, never mind," Mary said in frustration.

"There aren't any trains anywhere around here," Rhonda said. "There aren't even any train tracks. I don't know what you're hearing, but it's not a train."

"I don't know what it is," Mary said. Her disappointment showed on her face as she looked down at the floor again. "But it's something. I'm not making it up. Even that old guy at the nursing home said he heard it. Even told me a story about it."

Rhonda began to say something, but Mary interrupted her curtly. "Never mind." She swiped the back of her hand outwards as if swatting Rhonda away.

"I'm sorry I can't hear what you're hearing," Rhonda said.

Mary did not respond. She was irritated with herself for pointing out the whistle to her. She stood and walked into the kitchen and looked around.

"You hungry?" Rhonda asked.

"Nah," Mary answered. "I'm just thinking of all the stuff I have to do, all the stuff I have to buy for the apartment." She swept her eyes across the counters. "Like a coffee maker," she said. "I'm going to need coffee in the morning."

"Well, Walmart is open twenty-four hours," Rhonda said. "Go get one."

"Yeah," Mary said. "I will." She walked to the kid's room and looked in the door. Mary's shoulders visibly slumped, and her head dipped. She walked to her own bedroom and looked in. She stood staring into the room for several seconds. Her posture slipped with each passing second. She finally tucked her hands in her front pockets and let her chin fall to her chest. She stood that way for a few moments, straightened and joined Rhonda back on the sofa. She folded her arms in front of herself and slouched down.

"I have to go to work in a few minutes, so I've got to go home and change," Rhonda told her. "You going to be OK?"

"Yeah," Mary said. "I'm fine. I'll get used to this."

Rhonda stood. She felt reluctant to leave her sister but had no choice. "OK," she told Mary. "Call me on my cell if you need me."

Rhonda moved to the apartment door when Mary stopped her. "Rhon," she said. "Would it be alright if I came down to the chapel tonight?"

Rhonda shrugged her shoulders. "Why?"

"I think I'd like someplace to pray," Mary answered without looking at her.

"OK," Rhonda said as she mentally processed what Mary had just said. "I suppose so. You sure you're OK?"

Mary nodded. "I'm fine. It's just that I went to a different church Sunday and I've been feeling a need to pray. I think that would be a good place."

Rhonda stood at the door with one hand on the handle as she hesitated and looked at Mary. Mary appeared completely dejected. All of the spirit had left her. "OK, then," Rhonda said. "I'll see you at the home, but you call me if you need me, OK?"

"OK," Mary said as if her mind was a thousand miles away.

Rhonda hesitated only briefly to look back at Mary before she left the apartment. Mary appeared to be lost in thought as she watched the world outside her window. Rhonda nodded in understanding and closed the door behind her.

Chapter 9

After chatting with Rhonda briefly, Mary made her way to the chapel. She noticed that the door to the old man's room across the hall was closed. She looked in the chapel door window to be sure no one was already using it. It was empty. She went in and again sat on the edge of the same chair she had used the last time.

She looked up at the cross on the wall. She felt exhausted. Sadness passed through her in waves. She could feel herself crashing deeper into depression with each passing moment. She moved to the small kneeling bench at the front and folded her hands together, resting them on the padded arm rest. Looking up at the cross, her eyes began to tear.

"I can't fix this," she said as she stared up at the cross. "I am so sorry. I can't fix this. I need Your help. Please put my family back together." Tears began to fall freely and she bowed her head and rested on her hands.

~~~~

Leaving the chapel for the evening, she let the door close slowly behind her. The old man's door was now open. She took one step away from the chapel door when she heard her name called out.

"Mary?"

She stopped. She did not feel up to another conversation with the old man.

"Mary?" the old man called out again.

She felt compelled to peek in the door, to at least say hello. As she stepped in the doorway, he said, "Turn on the light and come in." She flicked the light switch and moved in only a step. "Sit for just a moment, will you?" he asked.

"Hi, Mr. Blunt," she began.

He interrupted her, "Please. Call me Allie."

"Hi, Allie. I can't stay. I need to get home."

"Yesss," he said in a deep tone, drawing it out. Mary began to wonder if he was able to say 'yes' normally. "But you can stay for just a moment." He tapped the empty chair with his cane. Mary reluctantly stepped over to the chair and sat down on its edge. She noticed a birthday card on the stand next to it.

"Is it your birthday?" she asked.

"No, it is not. I was born on Armistice Day."

"But you have a birthday card here."

"Yesss."

"Why?" Mary asked.

"What does it say?" Allie asked her.

She picked up the card, opened it and read it. "Happy Birthday. There's no signature."

"Yesss."

"So, why do you have a birthday card?"

"Perhaps someone forgot it here. Yesss. Perhaps someone sent it to me by mistake. Perhaps it was left here for you. It is not my birthday. I was born on Armistice Day. Yesss."

Mary set the card down on the table and settled back into the chair. "When is Armistice Day?" she asked him.

"No one knows when Armistice Day is anymore. It is a day. I was born on it. Much pain," he said as he nodded his head. "Much pain. Yesss."

Mary held her breath as she wondered what she should say. He tapped her leg again with the white cane as he looked straight forward.

"How did you know it was me when I came out of the chapel?" Mary asked him.

"Perhaps it was because I could feel you there or perhaps it is because I like your perfume," he answered. "But I knew. I knew. Yesss."

"I think maybe you can actually see me," Mary said. She instantly regretted referring to his blindness.

"Perhaps you are correct," he said. "Sometimes I see more than I wish to, I think. Yesss. But I think I like the thought of your smell better."

Mary smiled. She had not put on any perfume today. Perhaps Allie was flirting a bit, she thought.

"Mary, I hear much pain in your voice. Why do I hear pain?"

"What do you mean?" she asked him.

Allie turned slowly to face her. Again, he seemed to be looking deeply into her eyes with his own blind, white eyes. "Are you in pain?"

"I feel fine. I'm not in pain," Mary answered him.

"But you have been crying, haven't you? Yesss." Allie emphasized the 'yes.'

Mary tried to answer with a bold 'no' but choked on the word. She asked weakly, "How could you know that?"

"Yesss."

"How could you know that?" she asked again. Her voice was almost pleading. Her eyes began to tear again.

"You *are* in pain. Yesss." Allie said as he tapped her shin again with his cane. "Why are you in pain?"

Mary began to cry again. Twice she tried to speak, but the words froze in her throat. Allie reached out a shaky hand toward her. She reached out and took it, holding it gently. He stretched his cane out and tapped a box of tissue paper on the stand next to her and gently pushed it closer to her. She pulled a tissue out and wiped her face.

"Yes," he said. "Yesss."

Allie let several moments pass as he waited for Mary to calm herself. He finally released her hand and asked her again, "Mary, why are you in pain?"

"Be... Because I screwed up. I've destroyed my marriage. My whole life is in ruins."

"Yesss."

"There's nothing I can do to fix it. It's all gone now." Mary began to weep again.

"Yesss."

They sat quietly as Mary tried to gather herself again.

"What did you do, Mary?" he asked. Mary felt a deep compassion in his voice.

Mary wiped her eyes again and looked at him. Allie was staring straight ahead again. He prompted her by reaching out and tapping her leg with his cane. "I cheated on my husband," she said. "I didn't mean to. I got drunk, and things just happened. Someone gave my husband a video of me with the guy."

"Yesss," he said without judgment.

"Now my husband hates me and is going to divorce me. I am so sorry. I really messed things up. My kids are going to hate me. It can't be fixed."

"Yesss," Allie said as he nodded his understanding.

"I don't want to get divorced. I still love my husband, but I can't stop him. I screwed up."

Allie remained looking straight ahead and said softly, "yesss."

"I hurt so badly now I don't know what to do," she continued. "Every time I think, I think about how I messed up and how bad things are. I came here to the chapel to pray because I don't know what else to do. I came here to pray. There's nothing else I can do."

"Yesss," he said as he turned to face her again. "There is always something. That is something. Perhaps that is the best thing. Yesss."

Mary waited a moment. She could feel her hands trembling. "I keep asking God for forgiveness, but everything is lost," she said as she wiped her eyes again. "It's all gone. It can't be fixed." Allie continued to face her. Mary could not find the strength to look back.

"I was born on Armistice Day," he said. "I know much pain. It will get better, but I must ask you a question: Did you tell your husband that you were sorry?"

"Yes, of course," she replied as she stiffened.

"Did you say you were sorry because of *your* loss or because you were truly sorry for his loss?"

Mary's eyes darted around the room as her mind frantically thought over the question. "What?" she asked.

Allie continued to face her but did not answer. Mary tried to answer the question, "I'm not sure what you mean."

"Yesss."

"I *am* sorry," she insisted.

"But why did you tell Adam you are sorry? You told God you were sorry. Why did you tell God you were sorry? Because you want him to fix it or because the wrong was so great? Yesss."

"It was wrong," she said meekly. "I know it was wrong. I screwed up."

"Should your husband be angry with you?"

Mary hesitated before answering. "Yes. He's a good man. He has a right to be angry with me."

"Then why did you tell him you are sorry?" Allie asked.

"Because I am," she said. Anger at the question was beginning to take root.

"You told me that everything was lost. Everything is gone. You said your kids are going to hate you. Did you tell your husband you are sorry because what you did was wrong or because of what *you* have lost?"

Mary relaxed and wiped her eyes again. "I suppose it's both."

"Mary," he began. "You cannot have both. You can feel sorry for what you have lost, or you can feel sorry for what you did to your husband, but if you do not choose your husband over your own loss then you *will* lose everything and everyone. Yesss."

"So, what am I supposed to do?" she asked hoarsely.

"Accept your loss. Yesss. But truly be sorry for the pain that has been caused to your husband. Your husband is hurting more than you."

"More than me?"

"Yesss."

"Do you know my husband?" Mary asked him.

"No. I do not. What I know is that he is also in pain. He hides his pain behind his anger, but his hurt goes deep. Very deep. Yesss."

"So, what should I do, call him up and say I'm sorry? I've already done that. He didn't want to hear it."

"Yes, you have," he said. "Yesss."

"So, what more can I do?"

"You are still trying to fix it, Mary. *You* cannot fix it. It's no longer yours to fix. Now it is in God's hands."

"So, what can I do?" Mary was nearly pleading with him.

"I now leave that to you and God," he answered. "Yesss."

Mary felt exasperated. The old man knew how to thrust a knife deep into her soul but did not even try to heal the wound. "Do you know pain like this?" she asked him.

"Yesss." He drew the 's' out into a snake-like hiss.

"What happened to you?" Mary asked him.

He faced forward without saying anything. A moment passed, and he tapped her leg again with his cane. "I'm still here," she said impatiently. "I'm waiting on you. What happened to you?"

He began softly. "I know pain, but perhaps I am not talking about what happened to me. I was born on Armistice Day. Yesss. That was the day the Great War ended in Europe. Perhaps my father was there." He stopped talking.

"OK," Mary asked. "Did he die there?"

"Yesss."

"So, is that your pain?" Mary prodded.

"No." He began rhythmically tapping the tip of his cane on the floor in a slow cadence. "No, that is not my pain. My father died on Armistice Day. The same day I was born. Yesss."

"But the war had ended. How was he killed?" Mary asked.

"Yesss. Men were still trying to kill each other up to the very last minute of the war. It is a very sad thing to be the last one to die in a war. Very sad. Yesss. But that is not my pain."

"OK," Mary prodded again. "So, tell me what your pain is?"

"I was born on Armistice Day. Yesss."

"You said that," Mary said impatiently.

He continued tapping his cane on the floor. "I will tell you a story. There was someone who was born on Armistice Day, like me. His father had been in Europe for more than a year. The pain is: everyone knows how to count. Yesss." Mary looked at him as he faced forward. There was no expression on his face.

"Oh," said Mary softly. "So, he wasn't your father."

"Perhaps the boy I am speaking of was not me. Yesss. But the man was the only father the boy ever knew," he replied. "I was born on Armistice Day." He sat quietly. Mary thought he was through with his story when he continued again. "When they found the soldier, he was clutching a pistol in one hand and a letter in his other. In the letter, the boy's mother had tried to explain her infidelity. The soldier died one minute before the armistice was to take effect. He died of a single gunshot wound to his head. He was called a hero for his country. The last American to die in the great war. Yesss."

"I'm sorry," Mary told him.

Allie turned to face her again. His eyes blinked rapidly over the empty whiteness of his blindness. He continued to tap his cane on the floor. The cadence was growing increasingly faster. "Mary, do you know what they used to call people who were born like the baby boy in this story?"

Allie gave her a moment to answer. "Yes." She waited a moment more and then added. "A bastard."

The old man abruptly stopped tapping his cane. "Yesss," he said as he looked away from her again. "I do not like that word, Mary. It is given to the innocent. It is used to assign guilt and shame that does not belong to the child. It is not the child's sin." He paused and spoke more slowly. "Yesss, I have seen pain. Yesss."

Allie paused again and hung his head. "His mother died young," he said softly. "She loved the soldier. She died of a broken heart. Yesss."

"How old were you when your mother died?" Mary asked.

Allie lifted his head slowly. "Perhaps the story is not about me. Yesss," he said.

"So, what happened?"

"The boy lived." His lips were pressed tightly together, and he furrowed his eyebrows. "Mary, when I told you that his father died a hero for his country, you said you were sorry. Why are you sorry that they called him a hero?"

"I'm not sorry he was a hero. I'm sorry for what your mother did to him."

"Perhaps Mary, she was not my mother, but yesss, it was wrong," he said. "Yesss. But why are *you* sorry?"

Mary thought for a moment. "I'm just expressing that I feel bad for the man and you or whoever that little boy was. That had to have been tough."

"Yes. Tough. Yesss." He faced Mary again. His blind white eyes felt as if he was looking into her soul. "That is the sorry you must show your husband."

She tried to look back into his cataract covered eyes. The bright milky whiteness reflected her image back to her. She began to feel weak under his stare and turned away.

"It's all gone now," she said.

"Yesss."

"Yes," Mary repeated.

Allie tapped her leg again with the cane. "I am tired now," he said. "Perhaps we can talk the next time you come to pray. Yesss."

"OK. Perhaps."

"Yesss."

Mary stood and pulled another tissue from the box. She wiped her eyes as she stepped over to the doorway. "Good night, Allie," she said.

"Yesss."

Mary walked slowly down the corridor toward the exit. Deep in thought, she nearly passed the nurse's station without noticing.

"Mary? You alright?" Rhonda's voice startled her out of her thoughts.

"Yeah. Thanks, Rhonda." Mary gave her a short wave of her hand. "I'll see you later."

Mary exited the building and walked to her car. There seemed to be no breeze at all tonight. The world was silent around her. Just as she pressed the button on the key fob to unlock her door, she heard the train whistle. Two short and one long. It seemed louder tonight.

Chapter 10

Mary compared her grocery list against what she already had in her nearly full cart. The last thing she needed to complete her list was milk. The cart was harder to push now and pulled hard to her left. She leaned her body weight into it to keep it moving in the right direction. She missed the times when Adam would come along with her shopping. He would push the cart and tend to Kara while Aric kept busy running items back to the cart for her. Those times had been good times even on the days when the kids were not cooperating.

She pushed the cart to the end of the aisle and turned toward the dairy section. As she passed an adjacent aisle, she happened to look over and see Melissa looking over breakfast cereals. Mary had not talked to her since the wedding reception. She stopped her cart and stared down the aisleway.

Mary could remember that Melissa had been with her at the reception but nothing more from that night. She felt she should apologize to Melissa for her behavior the last time they were together. From the video that Adam had shown her it did not appear that she had been nice to her.

She instantly felt her anxiety spike and her breathing became shallow and fast. She felt her body flush. Turning the cart down the aisle, she tried to put on a smile before Melissa saw her. Melissa was oblivious to her approach as she reached up to the top shelf to pull down a cereal box. Mary stopped her cart behind her.

"Hi Melissa," Mary said meekly.

Melissa had just put her hand on the box but lowered it again in surprise at hearing Mary's voice. Instantly Melissa's face pinched in anger. "What do you want?" she asked angrily.

The tone of Melissa's voice stunned Mary, and her anxiety rose another notch. "I just wanted to say hi," Mary responded, "and I wanted to say I'm sorry if I behaved badly at the reception."

Melissa laughed out loud. "You've got to be kidding me!"

"I'm sorry, but I don't remember anything from that night, and I'd just like to be sure you and I are OK."

"You and I?" Melissa retorted as she took a step closer to Mary. "There ain't no you and I anymore. I don't want to have anything to do with you."

Mary was stunned into silence. Melissa paused for a moment then added, "And I really doubt that you don't remember anything. You acted like a whore." Her voice became louder with each word she spoke. "You are a whore! Adam didn't deserve what you did to him! You! Are! A! Whore!" Melissa nearly shouted the words as she leaned in toward Mary. Her face contorted in anger.

Mary dropped her hands from the cart and took a step back to add distance between her and Melissa. Her mouth hung open in shock. Melissa furrowed her eyebrows at her, lowered her voice and asked, "Who are you sleeping with now? Is it still Gabe or have you moved on to someone else? Or maybe you moved on to several people already." She paused a beat and then added coldly, "whore."

Mary was speechless. This was not the response she had expected. She had tried to apologize but Melissa attacked her in return. She looked away from Melissa and down the aisle. Several people were staring at her. She turned to look over her shoulder behind her. More people were focused on her. She looked again at Melissa who glared angrily at her. Melissa had clenched her jaw and was breathing fast and loudly through her nose.

Mary took another step back and then another. She turned quickly and rushed down the aisleway again. The people she passed turned to watch her go as she swept by them.

Melissa shouted after her, "I will never be friends with a whore!"

She walked as quickly as she could to the exit, almost running into the exit door before they could part for her automatically. On the other side of the door, her quick walk became a fast jog. She opened her purse and looked in as she fumbled for her keys. A car blew its horn at her and snapped to a stop as she jogged into its path. She only took a second to notice the car that had almost hit her, but she did not stop. When she reached her car door, she stopped and found her keys. Using the key fob to unlock it, she hurriedly climbed in and started the car. She put the car in reverse and looked over her shoulder.

Before taking her foot off the brake, she stopped and intentionally slowed herself down. She faced forward again and took several deep breaths. She could feel her heart pounding in her chest. As soon as she felt she had calmed herself enough to drive, she backed out of the parking space and headed back to the apartment.

At the apartment complex, Mary parked her car in her usual space in front of her building. The six blocks it took her to drive home had calmed her, but now she felt as if she were sinking fast into mental darkness. She walked slowly down the steps to her apartment, unlocked the door and stepped inside. She tossed her keys on top of the kitchen table where they slid across it and dropped to the floor on the other side. She hung her coat in the closet. In a daze, she walked to the sofa and sat down heavily in a slump.

"Whore." The word echoed in her mind.

"I am not a whore," she said out loud quietly.

"Whore." She heard Melissa say again.

"I am not a whore," she repeated.

"I will never be friends with a whore!" Melissa's words echo back to her.

"I am not a whore."

"Who you sleeping with now?"

Tears began to run down her face. "I am not a whore," she said again as she wiped her eyes and cheeks. She fought to hold the tears back, but the feelings overwhelmed her. She rolled to her side, then laid face down and wept.

Ralph Nelson Willett

Chapter 11

Mary stomped her feet heavily as she entered Forsythe Rehabilitation and Nursing Home. She brushed off the snow that had accumulated on her heavy coat and knitted hat. Looking up the hallway toward the opposite side of the building, she could see that it was empty of any people. Usually, there was at least one person walking up and down the hallway, even at this late hour.

She walked to the nurse's station and met Rhonda behind the counter. "Hi," she said startling Rhonda.

"Well, hey," Rhonda replied with a grin. "Haven't seen you in a couple of weeks. You doing OK?"

"Yeah, I'm fine. Sorry I haven't been around. I thought I'd come down and see you and use the chapel if that's OK."

"That's fine. I'll be getting off in an hour it you'd like to do something," Rhonda told her. "How's Adam and the kids doing?"

"The kids are fine. Adam still hates me. It's all he can do to talk to me when we swap the kids. He is still so angry. He'll never forgive me."

"Has he said anything more about the divorce?"

"No, he hasn't," Mary replied. "The way he acts I'm a bit surprised. I thought he was going to file at the end of last month as sort of a cruel Christmas/Happy New Year's present. He didn't. I don't know what's holding him back."

"Who knows," Rhonda said. "I hope he doesn't keep dragging it out for you."

"Me too," Mary said.

The phone rang, and Rhonda answered it. Mary mouthed the words to her, "I'm going to the chapel," and walked away. When she turned the corner, she saw Allie's door was open. She stepped into the doorway thinking that at this hour she would find him in bed asleep. As her eyes adjusted to the dim light, she saw him sitting in his chair. He was facing toward the wall. His lap blanket stretched across his legs and his white cane laid on top of it. She debated if she was up to a conversation with Allie or not.

"Who is standing there?" Allie asked as he tilted his head upward. His voice seemed kind and gentle.

Mary said nothing for a moment then said, "Hi, Allie."

Even though he faced away from her, she felt Allie's face instantly brightened. He turned his head to look at her with a smile so broad it seemed to make him glow in the dim light. "Mary!" he said happily. "Please, turn on the light and sit for a moment."

Mary turned on the light and sat down on the edge of the chair.

"Is it cold out?" Allie asked.

"Yes. Typical for late January."

"What is today?" Allie asked.

"Friday," Mary said.

"The date, Mary. Yesss," he said.

"It's the twenty-eighth," she said. "Almost February."

"I lose track of time," Allie said. "How deep is the snow now?"

"Not too bad. In some places, it's a couple of feet."

"I love winter," Allie said. "Yesss."

"Not me. I'd rather have summer."

"I have not seen you in a while. How have things been? Yesss."

"I've been OK."

"And your children?"

"They've been good, too," she said. "Aric is doing well in school, and Kara likes her day care."

"Daycare. Not mother. Yesss," Allie said. "How is Adam?"

"He's still very angry with me. He can hardly talk to me when we hand off the kids to each other."

"Has he asked you for a divorce yet? Yesss."

"No, not yet," she answered. "I don't know why he hasn't."

"Will you ask *him* for a divorce?"

"No. I'd still like to work things out."

"Yesss," Allie said. "Work things out. That would be good. Yesss."

"We'll see."

They sat silently for a moment until Allie said, "I like the way you smell today."

"I don't know what you're smelling," she said with a laugh. "I'm not wearing anything."

He grinned at her broadly. "There is a smell of happiness, Mary. You smell happy. Yesss."

"Maybe I am happier today. I've made a couple of new friends at the new church I'm attending."

"Do I hear music?" Allie asked as he tilted his ear up.

Mary listened. "No. I don't hear any music."

"Perhaps you have carried some music with you from your new church. I like it. Yesss."

Mary laughed again. "Carried some music? That's funny," she said. "I did like the music. They had a full band. Our old church only sang old hymns."

"Old hymns are good," Allie said nodding. "Yesss."

"But I like the new stuff better," Mary said.

"New is also good," Allie said. "Praise is praise. Yesss."

Again, they sat in silence for some time. Allie tapped her once on the shin with his cane. "I'm here," she said.

"I know you're here, Mary," he said. "Yesss. But, where are you?"

"Oh, I'm sorry," she said. "I'm here. I just drifted for a moment."

"Yesss."

"I saw the woman that was in Adam's video when I went shopping this week. She was a bridesmaid like me. She used to be my friend."

"Now she is not?" asked Allie.

"No. She was mad at me for what happened at the wedding. She called me a whore right to my face."

"Yesss," he said.

"I'm not a whore."

"You are not," replied Allie solemnly.

"She used to be my friend."

"Yesss."

"I asked her to forgive me, but she just laughed at me."

They sat silently for several seconds until Allie spoke thoughtfully. "She will be your friend again, Mary. Yesss."

"I doubt it," Mary said. "I think it's too late for that. I've lost a lot of friends. Everyone that used to be friends with both Adam and me won't have anything to do with me. I've lost all of them. Whenever I see them, it's like they don't want to talk to me or even know who I am. People can be so unforgiving."

"Yesss."

"It's hard, you know?" asked Mary.

"Yesss, I do know. Yesss," Allie said. "There is much to forgive. Yesss."

"I think it will be a long time before they forgive me if they ever will."

"I did not say that they need to forgive *you*, Mary. Yesss."

Mary squinted at him. "What do you mean?"

"There is much for you to forgive. You must prepare your heart. Yesss."

Mary stared blankly at him. Allie raised his chin as if he were looking off into the distance ahead of him. "What does that mean?" Mary asked again.

Allie did not respond. Mary waited patiently for him to speak. After several seconds Allie tapped her leg with his cane. "It is late, and I am tired now, Mary. Yesss."

"OK," she replied. "I need to go into the chapel and pray for a few minutes."

"Yesss, Mary," he said softly. "You must pray."

Ralph Nelson Willett

Chapter 12

Adam watched Kara and Aric in the living room from where he sat at the kitchen table. He rested one arm on it as he sat sideways to it. The Eleventh of March made it exactly five months since the wedding. He focused on the large envelope he held in front of him with sad eyes. Within the envelope were the papers that began the divorce process. His lawyer had instructed him to deliver the papers to Mary. She would give them to her lawyer, and the divorce process would finally begin. The papers would tell Mary what he wanted when their marriage dissolved. He tried carefully to be fair in dividing things up equally. She would get half of everything. It included money from the sale of the house, the 401K and joint custody of Aric and Kara.

It had taken Adam almost the full five months before he had his lawyer draw up the divorce papers. He was not sure why he had waited so long. He had told her the day after the wedding that he was going to file, but even now, with the papers in his hands, his mind searched for reasons to put it off.

Leaving his elbow on the table, he held the envelope up from one corner and let it swing back and forth. He measured the weight of it in his hands. He spun it between his fingers by its corners and looked at it from every angle. He had already signed the papers inside. Now he only had to give them to Mary. It was something that he was not anxious to do.

When he packed Mary's belongings for her, he had found their wedding album. He remembered that day clearly. She was four months pregnant with Aric at the time. The wedding had been hastily organized, but it was still beautiful. He leafed through the album. He had felt like crying then, but no tears came. The memories brought a crushing pressure of sadness on his chest. As he turned the last page of the album, the video of Mary kissing Gabe rushed back into his mind. He angrily snapped the album shut and shoved it hard into the moving box. He never wanted to see it again.

With a renewed passion, he had packed the remainder of her things and stacked them in the living room. He had expected Mary to be there within the next hour. Pulling a can of soda from the refrigerator, he sat in a chair on the front porch to wait. His anger had not abated by the time she arrived. She brought two friends that he had never met before to help her take her things. Tension grew inside of him as each box was removed from the house and stacked in the bed of the truck. By the time Mary left he was so angry he was shaking as he watched them drive away. Now, four months later, sadness filled his soul as he toyed with the envelope of papers that would legally and irrevocably divide them.

Adam struggled with the decision. He had always thought of divorce as wrong. That had been ingrained in him from his church upbringing. Now he was unsure. His understanding was that adultery was the one thing that the Bible allowed as a basis for divorce. Everyone he talked to agreed that it was alright for him to file for a divorce. Even his minister had advised him to dissolve the marriage. What he did not understand was why he felt so reluctant to give her the papers.

He ticked off a mental list of why he should divorce her:
- She had an affair.
- She could no longer be trusted.
- She had an affair.
- She was no longer physically attracted to him.
- She had an affair.
- She was physically attracted to someone else.
- She had an affair.

He felt a queasiness in his stomach as he tried to think of a reason why not to divorce her. Nothing came to mind.

But he did feel something though, something that was hidden deep inside of him that wanted to come out, fought to come out. A vision of her smiling face looking up at him at some random point in their lives together flashed through his mind. His eyes began to tear. He knew what that something was. It was the one thing that made him hesitate to give her the papers. It was probably the only thing that mattered; he still loved her.

He knew he still loved her. As hard as his anger tried to burn that fact away, it would remain true. It would *always* remain true.

He had already had opportunities to move on. A month earlier a woman had approached him in the church.

"Hi," she said as she met him in the aisle after the service. "Can I talk to you?" She indicated that she wanted him to sit down with her for a moment.

"I need to get my kids from children's church," he told her.

"It will only take a second," she said smiling.

He sat down next to her on the edge of the pew and faced her. Many people that knew about his separation had tried to console him. He thought this was one of those times. He would give her the moment she needed to do that.

"I understand you're available," she told him.

"What?" he asked in surprise. "What do you mean?"

"You're separated from your wife."

"Yes," he answered. He now felt uncomfortable.

"I know it's forward of me, but I've had my eye on you for a long time," she said smiling gently at him. "I'd like to ask you out."

Adam was stunned. His mouth hung open, and he did not know how to respond. Dating again had not crossed his mind. He felt uncomfortable and embarrassed. He looked around the sanctuary to see if anyone was watching them.

The woman was indeed beautiful. She had long auburn hair that fell past her shoulders in soft curls. Her skin had a smooth, silky texture. Her soft blue eyes were deep and sparkled at him when she spoke. He had not known much more about her other than she was divorced herself.

"I'm not divorced yet," he said.

"I know. But you're separated. I know your wife had an affair. I thought we could have dinner and just talk for a while."

The reminder of Mary's affair was like stirring hot coals, sparking his anger to life again.

He again looked around the room to see if anyone was watching and then faced her. She recognized his hesitation. "It's OK if you're not up for it. I understand," she said. "Maybe some other time."

"When did you have in mind?" he asked her.

"I was thinking perhaps tomorrow night," she said. "I'll treat you to a nice dinner."

He took only a moment to think it through. The kids would be with Mary this week. He had nothing going on, and dinner with a beautiful woman seemed a lot better than staying home alone in an empty house.

He nodded. "OK," he said. "I'll pick you up around six."

The woman's smile broadened. "I asked you out. I'll pick you up."

That made *him* smile. He had never been asked out by a woman before. He had always been the one doing the asking. This could be a fun experience, he thought. "OK," he said. "It's a date." They had exchanged cell numbers and emails. He gave her his address and she entered it into her phone.

"Great," she said. "I'll see you tomorrow night."

The remainder of that Sunday afternoon and evening he had eagerly looked forward to the upcoming date. He fantasized scenes where the two of them laughed together over dinner. They would hold hands as they walked downtown together in the cold February night air. They would sip hot chocolate together at a cafe while he charmed her. His wit would warm her to him and the evening would end with a passionate kiss at his door.

But that night a dream had awakened him from a sound sleep. Although he could not remember the dream, it left him shaking and feeling intensely guilty. All he could remember was that he had *had* a dream. He lay in bed restlessly for nearly two hours, unable to sleep. Finally, he sat up on the edge of the bed and hung his head. He could not go through with the date. The thought of it haunted him with guilt.

He picked up his iPad and drafted an email to the woman explaining that he did not feel right about dating at this time. Perhaps after the divorce is final, he wrote. Pressing the send button gave him relief, and he was able to sleep again. That had been almost a month ago.

A voice startled him out of his memories. "Are you OK, Dad?" Aric asked. Adam realized that his eyes were teary and wiped them before looking down at his son.

"Yeah," he answered. "I'm fine. Thank you for asking."

Aric seemed to have matured over the last few weeks. He took shuffling between the house and the apartment without complaint. He was more helpful than ever with his little sister.

"Can I go outside?" Aric asked.

"Sure," Adam answered as he stood to join his daughter in the living room. Aric quickly put on his shoes and ran outside to play.

Adam slumped down on the sofa. Kara had been playing with some of Aric's toy cars on the floor. She climbed on his lap with one of them. "See my car?" she asked him.

"I do," Adam replied, "It looks fast."

"Yeah," she said as she snuggled back into his arms.

He held her in his arms for a few minutes until she eventually climbed off his lap and resumed playing on the floor again. His mind wandered back to the day of that wedding five months ago. That day played out over again in his memory. The first text message video that came to him had churned his stomach. He tried to call her and then sent Mary a text asking her to call him. There was no response. The text message where the video showed Mary passionately kissing Gabe caused him excruciating pain. Every part of his body seemed to hurt. The final text, the one with the video of Mary driving off with Gabe, was the final crushing blow. He sank to the floor on his side as his mind filled in the blanks. He was numb. He did not remember how long he had stayed there, but he knew it was a long time.

It must have been three in the morning when he realized that Mary was not returning home that night. He sat in his rocker/recliner and rocked slowly back and forth as he stared vacantly ahead in deep emotional anguish. At seven that morning, he woke the kids, packed them into the car and delivered them to his parent's house without explaining anything to anyone. He returned home and waited as he played the videos over and over.

Kara tapped him on his knee breaking him out of his thoughts again. She showed him another of the little cars she had been playing with. He picked it up out of her hands, looked it over and said "nice" as he handed it back to her. She returned to playing with the cars on the floor.

Adam felt as if he were in a fog as he watched Kara play. He shook his head to clear his thoughts, pulled out his cell and paged slowly through his contact list. When Mary's contact information came into view, he stared numbly at it. His mind brought him back to the meeting he had with his minister, and the memory of his words felt as if they were slicing into him. "It's OK to cut your losses," he had said. "End the marriage and move on." He stared at his phone while those words repeated over and over again in his mind. He shook his head again to clear it one more time as anger began a slow boil. The decision was clear. He pressed the contact button for Mary's cell and waited for her to answer. "Hi, it's me," he said into it. "I'd like to talk. Can you do dinner with me Thursday?"

Ralph Nelson Willett

Chapter 13

The phone call from Adam lifted Mary's spirits. He did not sound as angry with her as he had when they had talked over the phone in previous calls or even in person when they exchanged the kids. He was always courteous, but there was always an undertone of anger. It was the first time she had not sensed the anger in his voice, but what lifted her spirits the most was that he had asked her out. He wanted to talk. That was a good start, she thought. Maybe there was some hope after all. She said a quiet prayer of thanks.

She made herself a dinner from leftovers. Living alone seemed to mean that there would always be leftovers, she thought as she spread them out on the table. She had just sat down to eat when there came a light knock at the door.

She stood and looked through the peep hole. She gasped and took a step back when she saw that it was Gabe standing at her door. She stared at the door in disbelief.

A second knock. Mary debated with herself. Should she open the door to him or not? She opened the door.

"Hi, Mary," Gabe said. He stood at the door smiling at her. He wore a light blue polo shirt, dark slacks, and black soft soled shoes. He was holding a bottle of wine cradled in his arm.

"Hi, Gabe," Mary said. "What are you doing here?"

"I just wanted to tell you how sorry I am for what happened and to see if there was any way I could make it up to you."

"Thanks, Gabe," she said, "but there's nothing you can do."

"Can I come in?" he asked as he rocked the bottle of wine toward her.

"No. That's not a good idea," she told him.

A faint look of dejection passed over him. "Well at least let me take you out for dinner or some drinks. That's the least I can do."

"No, Gabe," Mary told him. "I haven't had anything to drink since the wedding. I can't go out with you."

Mary thought she saw anger momentarily flash in his eyes but it passed quickly, and he maintained his smile.

"OK," he said. "I understand. But I really do feel bad, and I'd like to make it up to you somehow if you'd let me."

"Thanks, Gabe. But there's nothing you can do. Now if you'll excuse me I have to go." She closed the door leaving Gabe standing outside. She looked through the peep hole again just in time to see Gabe mouth an obscenity as if he were angrily screaming it. He straightened his back, looked in both directions down the hallway and then walked away.

Mary felt herself trembling. How did he find her? How did he know where she lived now? So many questions ran through her mind that she had no answers to. She could only hope that he was not stalking her and that this was a one-time event.

~~~

Wednesday after work, she stopped at Walmart and picked up a card with the intent to give it to Adam when they met for dinner Thursday. At her apartment, she opened it up and tried to think of something to write in it, but the only thing she could write was "Dear Adam." No more words would come to her. She stared blankly at the inside of the card for several minutes. She wanted to tell him she was sorry. She wanted to tell him how much she missed him. She wanted to tell him that she loved him and that he was all she could think about, but no words came.

She had bowed her head and tried to pray. She prayed that God would give her wisdom during her dinner with Adam, but her prayer felt as if she were speaking to an empty room. Her words seemed to echo back at her from the walls. It was then that she decided to visit the nursing home chapel again.

Allie's door was closed when she turned the hall corner toward the chapel. She felt a twinge of disappointment. She had thought about their conversations several times throughout the last few weeks since she had last seen him. Now she was not sure if she was feeling the need to pray at the chapel or if she just wanted to visit with Allie.

She peered into the chapel door window. No one was inside. She stepped in, wrapped her coat around the back of a chair and moved immediately to the prayer bench. She folded her hands and looked up to the cross. She tried to pray, but no words came to her. The images of the night at the wedding reception raced through her mind crowding out all other thoughts. An image came to her of how Adam must have felt the moment he saw the first video, how hurt he must have been. She tried to envision how it would have felt had the roles been reversed. It caused her to tremble with emotional pain. She folded her hands and put them on the table in front of the kneeling bench and rested her forehead on them. Another image came to mind of Gabe standing in her doorway with a bottle of wine. She felt her trembling intensify with the thought of him.

"Hello, Mary."

The voice startled her causing her to jump. She quickly turned to see Allie standing just inside the chapel door. He was sweeping his cane back and forth in front of him as he walked slowly toward the front of the chapel.

"Allie, you frightened me," she said as she stood from the bench. She felt relieved that Allie had joined her. "I didn't hear you come in."

"Yesss." He found his way to an empty chair and sat down. He gripped the cane with both hands and stood it vertically in front of him on the floor. Mary turned a chair to face him and sat down.

"How did you know I was here?" she asked him.

"I knew. Yesss. I knew. Perhaps it was the sound of your footsteps."

"Your door was closed. How could you hear me coming?"

"Perhaps it's your perfume. Yesss. Your perfume."

"Allie," she said as she nearly giggled. "I'm not wearing any perfume."

"Yesss. There is a sweet smell that follows you, Mary. Yesss."

In the dim light of the room, she could see that Allie was smiling. The smile reminded her of her great grandfather when he would sit and watch the children play. It was a peaceful and contented smile.

"What are you praying for, Mary?" he asked.

"I come here to get away. It's quiet here."

"But you did not answer my question, Mary."

Mary thought a moment. She was still uncomfortable talking about prayer for some reason even though she was praying nearly every day now. The thought of telling Allie what she was praying for seemed overwhelming. "I couldn't pray tonight," she answered.

"Yesss."

"Do you pray?" she asked him.

"Yesss."

"What do you pray for?"

"You, Mary. Yesss. I pray for you." He reached out and tapped her leg once with his cane.

"But you don't know me," she replied. "Not really."

"Yes. I know you, Mary. Yesss." He tilted his face up toward the cross. "I know Mary. Yesss."

Mary automatically turned to face the cross with him. The room was quiet as they sat in momentary reflection. "What do you want to pray for, Mary? Yesss."

Mary faced him again. "I think I want to pray to have my husband back. I want my family back." She waited a beat and then added, "I want my life back."

"Yesss," Allie said. He spoke so softly and with a tone so deep that she almost did not hear him.

They fell into silence. Allie kept his face lifted toward the cross. Mary stared vacantly at the floor.

"What does your husband do?" Allie finally asked.

"He works for a credit union. He's a loan officer."

"Yesss," replied Allie. He drew out the 's' even longer than usual. "What does he *want* to do?" He turned slowly to face her. His smile was kind and gentle.

"What do you mean? I don't know," she answered.

"Yesss. But I think you do, Mary," he said. "What *did* he want to do?"

Mary thought for a moment. "Well, years ago he wanted to go into some type of church ministry."

"What happened? Why did he not go into church ministry?"

"Because of me."

"Yesss," he said as he faced the front of the chapel again. "Because of you. Yesss."

Again, the room fell silent as Mary resumed staring at the floor. To Mary, the silence was nearly unbearable. The passing seconds felt like hours. Allie spoke first. "How is it that because of you he now works for a credit union?"

Mary cleared her throat. This was not something she wanted to share with the old man. She looked at his face, and he turned slowly toward her. Again, those blank, white eyes seemed to look deeply into her, compelling her to answer. Her voice was soft and quiet as she told him her story. "We were both in our last semester in college when we met. He planned to go to seminary when he graduated. We found out a few weeks later that I was pregnant. We got married, and that's when Aric was born. He still wanted to go to seminary, but I talked him out of it. We had a family to take care of now, so he took the job at the credit union."

"Yesss," he said as he faced forward toward the cross again. "Yesss."

"That's why it's my fault."

"Is there another reason you didn't want him to go into church ministry?

Mary thought about it for a moment. "Yeah. I wasn't into church like he was."

"Yesss," Allie said. "Very true. Yesss. Is he happy being a loan officer?" he asked.

"I don't think so, but he doesn't complain."

"Yesss. He does not complain. But Mary, do you think he bears no fault of his own for not being happy?"

She thought about the question a moment. "I'm not sure what you mean."

"It took two of you to become pregnant. Adam also made choices. Did he not?"

"I suppose," she said.

"Were those the choices he was supposed to make?" he asked.

"Of course. We got married because we were going to have a baby."

"Yesss. Yes, you did have a baby. But was he called to go into the ministry?"

Again, she thought about her answer. "I suppose he thought so. But that isn't how life works. You have to make choices that are relevant to the moment. You have to work with the cards you're dealt."

"Mary, Mary, you cannot run from what God has called you to do. Yesss. Do you know the story of Jonah and the whale?"

"Of course. Every child knows that story." She could feel a tension rising in her again. She interpreted her tension as anger. "But that has nothing to do with us."

Allie began to rhythmically tap his cane on the floor. "You cannot run from God, Mary."

"I'm not running from God. If anything, right now I'm running *to* God. I'm going to a new church, and they're showing me how to actually know God. That's why I come here to pray. It's peaceful here like I feel when I'm at my new church. It just feels like God is here."

"God *is* here, Mary," Allie said. "Yesss. But you *have* run from God." The rhythm of the tapping began to pick up its pace, and he spoke more rapidly. "When you married, for whatever reason you married, you both connected your callings to each other; yours to his and his to yours. You have not done what God has asked you to do." He turned to face her quickly. The tapping stopped abruptly adding emphasis to his words. "Yesss."

She tried to look him in his white eyes but quickly looked away again. He had lost his smile, and now his face looked stern and taut, nearly angry. There was an instant tension in the air, and she felt as if she were withering beneath his stare. She realized she was holding her breath and felt sure she would have to force herself to exhale. The old man turned slowly away again and visibly relaxed. Mary felt the tension release from her as well as she exhaled.

The room remained silent until Allie tapped her leg with his cane. "What does God want from me?" she asked him softly.

"What are you running from?" Allie asked.

"I'm not running from anything."

"Yesss."

"I'm not."

"You told me you talked your husband out of going into seminary."

"We were starting a family," Mary protested. "That wasn't an option. How were we supposed to support ourselves?"

"Is it God who supports you or is it you that supports you? Yesss."

"What do you mean?" Mary asked.

"You know the answer to the question, Mary," Allie said. "Yesss."

"I suppose that it's God. He's the one that gave us the skills we have so we can support ourselves. He's blessed us in so many ways; good jobs, wonderful children, a wonderful place to live."

"Why are you here, Mary?" he asked her quietly.

"Where?"

"Here. In this chapel. Tonight. Talking with me. Yesss." His voice seemed to grow shakier as he spoke.

Mary thought a moment before answering. "I'm here because it's a good place to pray."

"Yesss," he said drawing it out with the familiar snake-like hiss.

"That's why I'm here," she said.

"What are you praying for, Mary?"

"For restoration. I want my husband and family back."

"What does God want?" he asked her.

"I'm sure he wants my family back together, too. Isn't that the right thing?" she asked incredulously.

"Yesss," Allie answered.

"That's all. We want the same thing; my family back together. That's what I'm praying for."

Allie's face was expressionless as he sat quietly facing the cross.

Long seconds passed in silence. Mary was feeling defeated. "What am I supposed to do?" she asked him. "I can't go back and undo what I did. We can't go back in time and go to seminary. What am I supposed to do?"

"Are you sure you know what *God* wants, Mary?" he asked her. "*You* may think it is better for your family to return to the way it was, but is that what God wants? Have you asked Him? Is that what He wants for you? Is that what you pray for, Mary, to know what God wants? Or do you only pray for what you want?" he asked. "Yesss."

Mary felt at a loss for words. She had been pleading with God to restore her family. It had never occurred to her to pray to understand what God wanted or what He wanted her to do. She felt ashamed as she answered him quietly, "I pray for what I want."

He turned his head to face her again. "Yesss," he said again in a low toned whisper. "I was born on Armistice Day but I have lived a very long time. It appears to me that you are trying to fix things when it is only God that can fix your marriage. But it all starts when you choose to stop running. Mary, will you stop running now? Will you stop being a Jonah? Yesss."

Mary used both hands to wipe her face and then pushed her hair back. She looked around the room as she thought about the question. Her eyes were drawn to freshly picked flowers that were arranged at the front of the chapel. For the first time, she noticed their scent. Perhaps it was because she noticed the flowers that she could now smell them, or perhaps she noticed them *because* of their scent. Her eyes lingered on them, unfocused. She let the colors blur together as the question ran through her mind. Was she running?

What was she running from? Was she ready to stop running?

"I don't know what I'm running from," she told Allie. "I don't feel any calling from God. That's Adam. I don't think I'm running away from anything."

"Yesss," he answered.

"Do you think I'm running away from something?"

"You need to ask God that question," he replied.

"I know you're not supposed to try and bargain with God, but do you suppose that if I tell God that I'll stop running from whatever it is that He wants, that He'll put my family back together?"

"You cannot bargain with God, Mary. No one can. You have nothing to bargain with. You have nothing He needs. You have nothing to purchase God's service to you. God needs nothing from anyone. Yesss."

Mary felt defeated and slumped in her chair. "Then I'm lost," she said. "I don't know what God wants, and I have nothing to offer to get my family back together."

"Ah," he said. "But you do have something to offer, but it is something you cannot use to bargain with. You can offer you. You can *only* offer you. It is you that He wants. All of you. Not just on Sunday, but all of you, all of the time. The you who tries to hide from Him, the you that has forgotten Him." Allie paused then added, "the you that has been running from Him. Yesss."

Mary felt the tears well up in her eyes and fought to push them back down. "OK," she said. "If I can figure out what God wants from me then I'll stop running."

"Yesss," said Allie as he stood. He made his way to the door and stopped to face her direction. "Mary, I was born on Armistice Day. I am older than the earth itself. You are young. Your life is not over. Find out what God wants you to do. Ask Him. Then listen for His answer. Choose to do what he asks of you even if it means releasing your desire for restoration of your family. Doing what God wants is more important than what you want. Yesss." He turned and left the room.

Mary sat quietly in her chair. She felt overwhelmed and weak. She felt sad and confused. She felt like crying.

The smell of the flowers caught her attention again, and she focused her eyes on the bouquet. The brightly colored flowers stood out in sharp contrast to the rest of the dark room making them seem to emit a light of their own. She saw a small card that appeared to be floating within the bouquet. Staring at the card for a moment, she finally stood and crossed the room to look at it. She touched the edge of the card and ran her finger along it. Pulling the card from the plastic stem that held it, she looked it over.

What had appeared to be a card from a distance was a small white envelope no larger than a business card. She opened it and pulled the contents out. It was a small yellow Post-it sticky note. On it was a brief note penciled in a childish scrawl. It said: "I miss you, Mom. I love you." It was signed by Ben.

Tears now welled up again as she thought about her own children. She felt crushed. She sat down on the nearest chair and held the note in her lap with both hands. She did not know where the flowers came from or anyone named Ben. She wondered what the circumstances were that prompted the flowers to be sent. Were they from some little boy whose mother was here, dying under hospice care? The thought consumed her. She envisioned a little boy the same age as Aric visiting his mother as she lay dying. In her mind, she saw the woman holding out her hand to the little boy and passing away just as he took hold of it. She could hear his voice cry out "no mommy, don't go, don't go." Tears rolled down her cheeks as she tried to force the visions from her mind.

Thoughts of missing her own children began to fill the void. A new vision came to mind. She could see herself holding little Kara's hand as clearly as if Kara had actually been right beside her. Kara looked directly up into her face and said, "Please don't go, Mommy." A quiet "Oh" escaped from Mary as the vision caused her to fold her arms across her stomach. As if in pain, she rocked forward and back as the tears rolled down.

Minutes passed as she held and rocked herself. Her vision blurred through the tears as she stared with unfocused eyes toward the front of the chapel. She glanced up at the cross. Slowly she rose and knelt again on the kneeling bench. She folded her hands together, closed her eyes, and rested her forehead on her arms.

"Father," she began. "I don't know what You want. I only have myself to offer You. I only ask one thing and I know I have no right to ask this and I have nothing to bargain with. I only ask that You take care of my family as I release them to You. Please don't let them ever forget that I love them very much. There's nothing more I can do except give myself to You. Please tell me what You want me to do."

Mary remained on the kneeling bench for several minutes until the tears finally stopped. She moved to a chair again and sat down. She realized she was still holding the little note from Ben. She read it once more and then returned it to the little envelope. She rolled the envelope over and over in the palm of her hand in a slow spin.

She felt drawn to open a little drawer that was in the table the bouquet sat on. There was a hard-covered Bible in it. She removed the Bible, opened it on her lap and leafed through random pages. The pages flipped open to Isaiah 55. Her eyes ran down the page until they stopped on verse 8. Someone had underlined the verse with a red ink pen.

"For My thoughts are not your thoughts, neither are your ways My ways," declares the Lord.

She read the verse again and then ran her finger under each word as she read it a third time. She looked up at the cross. She focused on it as if it were the first time she had seen it, as if its meaning had just been revealed to her, like a long-hidden secret. She bowed her head and closed her eyes. "Father," she said in a trembling voice. "I'll do whatever it is You ask me to do."

She did not know how long she remained there with her head bowed and eyes closed but now she felt at peace. She looked back up at the cross and bit her lower lip. The cross looked different to her somehow. It somehow seemed more… She thought about it for a moment. It somehow seemed more inviting.

The weight of the Bible on her lap caught her attention. It was still opened to Isaiah 55. She placed the little envelope between the pages of the Bible, closed it and then returned it gently to the drawer.

As she left the chapel, she saw that Allie's door was closed again. She crossed the hall and raised her hand to knock but stopped just short of actually knocking. Instead, she placed her palm on the door and brushed it across it. It felt cool to the touch and she could feel the texture of the paint. She remained there a moment and then began walking slowly away as she let her hand brush across the hallway wall.

Mary turned the corner and walked the long hall toward the exit. Rhonda saw her coming down the hall toward her. Mary appeared to be deep in thought.

"Are you alright, Mary?" Rhonda asked her.

Mary gave her a weak smile. "Yes. I'm fine. I'm just really emotional today."

"I understand. I get it. Is there anything I can do for you?"

"No. Thanks. I'll be alright. Goodnight."

"Goodnight, Mary," Rhonda told her. "If you need anything or just want to talk, you call me, OK?"

"Yes, I will," Mary answered. "Thank you."

She was almost to the exit when Allie came to her mind. "Yesss," she said quietly drawing it out as he did. "Yesss," she repeated. When she left the building, she felt weak and shaky. Reaching her car, she leaned back against the door and rested as she held her keys loosely in her hand. Small flakes of snow blew across the parking lot pavement in tiny, twisting streams. She heard the train whistle again. Two short and one long. Turning to face the direction it came from Mary listened for it again. She heard only the wind blowing through the bare branches of the trees.

Ralph Nelson Willett

Chapter 14

Mary watched Adam enter the restaurant from her booth. She had arrived five minutes earlier and had the waitress seat her at a booth where she could watch the door. Her heart sank as she saw Adam enter with a large envelope in hand. She could only think of one thing that could be.

"Hi," he said as he slid into the seat across from her. He set the envelope on the seat beside him.

"Hi," she replied with a trembling smile. "The kids with your folks?"

"Yeah, they are."

An awkward silence ensued.

"You look nice," he eventually said.

"Thank you," she replied. She had taken extra time to get ready to be sure she looked nice for him. She wore the blouse that Adam once said he liked, a pair of newer jeans and blue tennis shoes. She applied her makeup carefully, and it had turned out nice. She wanted to look nice for Adam, and she felt confident that she did.

"Your perfume smells good, too," he added as he pulled out two menus from the stand holding them, and handed one to her. She was surprised to hear him say he liked the smell of her perfume. She had not thought to put any on. Allie had said the same thing to her last night. She had not been wearing any then either. She wondered what they were smelling.

Adam began looking his menu over. The waitress stopped by with glasses of water and asked if they needed more time. Mary said that she did and continued looking over her menu as Adam had made his selection and put his menu back in the stand.

"What are you having?" Mary asked him.

"Taco salad," he answered as he let his eyes wander around the room. He appeared irritated.

Mary settled on a burger and then set the menu flat on the table in front of her to wait for the waitress's return.

"So," she began, "how have you been?"

"I'm good," he answered. "What about you?"

"I'm doing OK, I guess."

"How's the apartment?"

She shrugged. "It's an apartment. Not much else I can say about it," she answered.

The awkward silence returned. Moments passed slowly. Adam looked around the restaurant again and then finally looked directly at Mary. His face had a look of compassion. He opened his mouth to speak.

"I miss you," Mary blurted out, softly interrupting him before he said anything. She instantly regretted her impulse as Adam stiffened while inhaling deeply through his nose. He held his breath for a second and then blew it out through his mouth as his chest slumped. He pursed his lips together. Mary had promised herself that she was not going to say anything like that unless Adam had first, but the words spilled out of her.

She now felt committed to the direction she began the conversation with. She continued with a pained look on her face. "I wish there was something I could do to undo what I did. I am so sorry. There are so many things that I regret doing and *not* doing in our marriage. I've had a lot of time to think about things, and I just want to say I'm sorry."

"Mary," Adam said. "It's not just the affair. There's a lot of things."

"I know," Mary admitted. "I know I talked you out of your dream and I'm sorry. I know I have not been as responsive to you as I should have been. I know..."

"What dream?" he interrupted.

Mary felt surprised as if he should have already known the answer. "You wanted to go to seminary after college, even after Aric was born. I regret that I talked you out of that. That was wrong of me, and I don't blame you for resenting me for that."

Adam blinked at her as he processed what she just said. He appeared dumbfounded. He spoke slowly, deliberately choosing each word carefully. "I don't resent you for that," he said. "That was the right thing to do."

"Was it?" she asked. "I've been thinking about it. It's been bothering me. If God called you into ministry, then who am I to talk you out of it?"

"You're my wife," he answered. "We made that decision together. We had a baby, and we needed to take care of him. I needed a job. Seminary wasn't an option."

"I'm not so sure," Mary said. "Someone told me recently that if God calls you to something, then He'll provide a way for you to do it. I feel like I talked you out of doing what God wanted you to do."

Adam tried to take in what Mary was saying. He shook his head. "It's too late for that now," he said.

"Is it? Did God change His mind about what He called you to do?"

"It just didn't work out," he said uncomfortably.

The waitress came, took their orders and stepped away again.

Adam looked at her, leaned in and squinted one eye. "When did you start thinking like that?'

"Like what?" Mary asked.

"You don't normally talk about 'What God wants'," he said while flicking air quotes.

Mary grinned. "Just recently, I guess," she said. "I'm going to that new church by the expressway. I've learned a lot since I started there. I've also been going to the chapel sometimes where Rhonda works when I don't have the kids."

"Why?" he asked confused.

She shrugged. "I don't know. It's a quiet place to pray."

"You pray?"

"I've always prayed. Just not out loud." Mary was becoming a little more comfortable talking about praying.

Adam looked at her with a squint until she felt uncomfortable enough to look away. "I've been praying too," he said. "What are you praying for?"

Mary put her hands on her lap and leaned forward against the table. "For the kids. For me." She hesitated a moment and then added, "for you."

Adam cocked his head and grinned. "I've never heard you say you've been praying for me before."

"I'm sorry for a lot of things. That's one of them. And I'm really sorry for what happened to you."

"What happened to me?" Adam seemed to genuinely not know.

"What I did to you," she said quietly. She looked away, saddened.

A look of pain crossed his face. Mary hung her head.

"Well it did happen," he said softly. A compassionate expression came to his face again. "I'd like to talk about something else," he said. Mary looked into his eyes and smiled gently.

Out of Mary's view, Adam reached down on the seat and touched the envelope with the divorce papers in it. He picked up one edge, hesitated and set it down again. Her smile softened him. He ran his finger along the length of it, stopped again at its bottom edge and lingered there. He then pushed the envelope away from him another inch and then rested his arms back on the table.

Their conversation drifted from one subject to another, from how the kids were doing to how each of them was doing. They had finished their dinner, and the waitress had removed their plates. They were both enjoying each other's company. Their moods had been elevated. It was beginning to feel like when they first dated back in college, when Gabe stepped up to their table.

"Hi," Gabe said as he smirked down at them.

"Gabe!" Mary exclaimed in panic. "What are you doing here?"

Adam's eyes instantly reflected his anger. Gabe ignored him. "Is this your husband?" Gabe asked Mary as he nodded toward Adam.

"Yes," Mary told him trying to suppress her panic. "This is my husband, Adam."

Gabe turned to face Adam and stuck out his hand. Adam glanced at his hand but did not take it. He glared up at him. Gabe pulled his hand back and wiped it on the side of his shirt. He then focused his attention on Adam.

"You've got a wonderful little lady," he told Adam. Adam's eyes pierced Gabe with growing anger.

"Gabe," Mary said loudly. "You need to leave."

He ignored her and spoke again to Adam. "You're a lucky man. She's really nice." The smirk grew across his face. Adam only glared at him. "And really good in bed," he added.

"Gabe!" Mary shouted at him. "Leave! Now!"

Again, Gabe ignored her. He leaned in toward Adam and said, "I gave her twenty dollars for a really good time. How much does she cost *you*?"

Adam quickly swung his legs around and rocketed out of the booth. Gabe tried to lean out of his way but stumbled backward. Adam launched his fist straight from his shoulder and twisted his hips into the punch. He caught Gabe squarely in the mouth. Gabe stumbled another step back and fell with a heavy thud on the floor with his back leaning against the bench of the booth across the aisle.

Adam towered over him angrily. Both fists were clenched at his sides. Every muscle in his body coiled tightly like a wound spring ready to snap out. He was breathing loudly through his nose as if he had just run around the block.

Gabe was dazed. He looked out with crossed eyes. He shook his head to try and clear it. Slowly the fog cleared and he put his hand up to his mouth and spit two teeth into it. Anger swept over him, and he swore multiple times at Adam, calling him profane names.

"I'm calling the cops!" Gabe screamed at him. "I'm putting you in jail!" He started to try and stand, but

Adam stood in his way towering over him. "Move!" he screamed at Adam. Adam did not move. Gabe swore again, and again shouted "Move!" Adam took one step back to give him room to stand. Gabe pushed himself off the floor and looked at the bloody teeth he held in his hand. Gabe burst out again in profanity. Adam was poised to strike again. "I'm calling the cops!" Gabe shouted again as he began walking away from Adam backward. "I'm going to sue you for everything you've got!" He added another string of profane names. Adam took one step toward Gabe. Gabe turned quickly and rushed out of the restaurant, pushing a much larger male patron at the door to one side.

Adam relaxed his body as he watched Gabe through the window. Gabe rushed to his car in the parking lot. Adam sat down across from Mary again. She looked terrified. "He had that one coming," Adam said as he looked over the broken skin of his knuckles.

"He's going to call the cops," Mary said in a panic.

"Let him," Adam said while calmly wiping his knuckles with a napkin. "If I go to jail, you come and bail me out. OK?"

Mary blinked at him in a daze. "OK," she said stunned.

The manager of the restaurant walked up to their booth. "I need to ask you to leave," she said.

Mary and Adam slid out of the booth and walked up to the cash register together where Adam paid the bill. Mary noticed he had tucked the envelope back under his arm. She still wondered if he was going to give it to her. Adam only said, "I'll talk to you later," as he gave her a hand wave and casually walked to his car. Mary wondered how he could be so calm after what just happened. He backed his car out of its parking space and drove off.

Mary realized that she was standing on the sidewalk opened mouthed, watching him drive away. She climbed into her car, closed the door behind her and placed both hands on the top of the steering wheel. She still felt stunned at the fast turn of events. As she calmed herself she began to feel relieved. She had seen Adam walk in with the large envelope and felt she knew what he wanted to talk about but instead, it turned out to be a pleasant dinner. That was until Gabe showed up. She closed her eyes and said a brief prayer of thanks. When she opened her eyes, she heard the train whistle again, two short and one long.

~~~

Turning the corner toward the chapel, Mary found the door opened to Allie's room. She knocked at the door and peered into the darkness. "Hello?" she inquired.

"Hello, Mary," returned Allie's voice. "You sound well today."

"I'm feeling well. Can I come in?"

The God Whistle

"Yes, of course," he answered. "Please turn on the light and make yourself at home. You are always welcome here." Allie sounded cheerful.

Mary stepped in and sat on the vinyl chair next to him. He reached out and tapped her leg once with his cane. "Something has changed, Mary," he said. "What is it?"

Mary chuckled at him. "How could you know that? I've only said a couple of words to you."

"Perhaps it's your perfume," he responded with a smile. "You smell happy today."

She could not help but smile. "Yeah, that must be it. I'm wearing happy perfume."

"Ah, yesss," he said drawing out the yes into a long hiss. "Happy perfume. It smells so nice. I like happy perfume. Yesss. So, tell me, Mary, what has changed?"

"Adam and I had dinner together last night. It went well." She was smiling broadly at him.

A smile slowly spread across Allie's face and grew until it showed his bright white teeth. "That is good, Mary. Yesss. That is very good. Yesss. So tell me Mary, what happened last night that makes you so happy today?"

"It was just a good dinner. It was almost like a date. He didn't seem as angry with me. We talked a long time about how the kids were and how he was doing. It felt like he still cared for me. That might be a little too much to hope for, but that's what it felt like."

"Yesss," Allie said. "Did you talk about getting back together?"

"No. We didn't talk about that. I was just glad to hear that he was doing well. I get the kids every other week, so I know they're doing OK, but I was glad to know he's doing OK, too."

"Yesss. That is good, Mary."

"You know what he said?" Mary asked him. "He said my perfume smelled great. That was funny. He sounded like you when you say I smell happy. What's funny is I almost never wear perfume, and I wasn't last night. I don't know what you guys are smelling, but at least you seem to like it."

"Ha!" he said. "The sweet perfume of the one I love twill ever cross my mind. No greater gift a man should have than his true love he should find. Yes!" His 'yes' was short and sounded enthusiastically happy.

"OK," she said. "Who's that quote from?"

"I do not know, Mary. Perhaps I made it up. Yesss." He was grinning from ear to ear as he faced the doorway. He turned to face her. He seemed to glow. His eyes were closed as he turned to her.

Mary returned a smile he could not see. He reached out his hand shakily to her, and she took it. They remained quiet, taking in the moment.

"I see you still have all your teeth," Mary told him, trying to keep the conversation going. Allie's teeth seemed unusually white. She had at first thought them to be false teeth but the gap in the upper teeth suggested otherwise. "Are those still your real teeth? They look pretty white for someone your age."

"I was born on Armistice Day," he told her. "But these are my real teeth. I have them all. Yesss."

"So, what's the secret to keeping all your teeth all those years?" Mary asked him.

"Keeping away from other men's wives, to start," he answered. His smile grew broader still.

"That's funny," she said.

"But true. Yesss." He gave her hand a gentle squeeze then released her.

"So, you heard what Adam did," she stated as she wondered who could have told him about what happened the night before.

"No, Mary. What did Adam do?" Allie asked.

"He knocked Gabe's teeth out," she said with a grin.

"Why did Adam knock Gabe's teeth out?"

"Because he called me a whore," Mary said still grinning. "I've never seen Adam move so fast in his life.

He punched Gabe right in the mouth and knocked him down."

"Ah!" Allie said nearly cheering. "That is good. Yes!" Again, Allie used the short, happy yes.

"I saw Gabe spit two of his teeth out."

"You see? That is why I still have all my teeth. I do not say things like that about the wife of another man."

"Gabe said he was going to call the cops and then he was going to sue Adam for everything he owned. The cops never showed up. I'd bet he will try and sue, though."

There was a moment of silence. The smile left Allie's face, and he became serious again. "I do not think he will, Mary. Yesss."

Again, a moment of silence this time broken by Mary. "I was going to tell you that the last time I was here I heard the train whistle again," she told him. "And I heard it last night when I was leaving the restaurant."

"Yesss," he replied. "Two short and one long. He is coming but already here. Yesss."

"Do you think it's a real train?"

"Something is real. Yesss. It is very real."

"So, do you believe in ghosts?" she asked him.

He smiled broadly at her. "Ghosts? What are ghosts? Perhaps it is a moment trapped in time that only you can see. Perhaps it is a message from God. Yesss." He waited a moment and then smiled broadly at her again. "Perhaps it is something we will never know the answer to. Yesss."

Again, there was a moment of silence. Allie then spoke quietly. "Did you ask God what He wanted of you? Yesss."

"Yes, I did."

"Yesss. And what does He want of you, Mary?" asked Allie.

Mary was silent for a moment as Allie faced her. He tapped her once on the leg. "I don't know what He wants me to do. How is He supposed to tell me?"

Allie began tapping his cane on the floor in a slow rhythm as he waited for Mary to continue.

"So I prayed that God would show me what to do. Now what, Allie?" Her voice felt weak.

"The happiness has left your voice, Mary. Yes."

"I know," she replied. "Does God ever talk to you, Allie?"

"Yesss."

"So, what does He say?" she asked him.

"He says to take care of you, Mary. Yesss." The cane continued to tap slowly.

Mary almost chuckled at him. "How are you supposed to take care of me?"

"I am here, Mary. Yesss."

"So how are you supposed to help me?"

"I am here, Mary," he repeated. "Yesss." He stopped tapping the cane on the floor and touched her leg with the cane. "I am here. You are here. There is so much more. Put the happy back in your voice, Mary. You *will* know what God wants of you. Yesss."

There was an uncomfortable silence in the room again. "Tell me a joke, Mary," he said.

Mary's thoughts instantly shifted. "Tell you a joke? I don't think I know any jokes."

"Tell me one about the chicken crossing the road. Yesss."

"OK. Why did the chicken cross the road?"

"Why, Mary? Why did the chicken cross the road?" He was smiling broadly again.

"To get to the other side." Mary could not help but smile back at him.

"Ha!" He said. "That was funny. You tell a good joke, Mary. Yes!" He spoke quicker than usual, and there was a distinct pleasure in his voice.

"Allie, you can't tell me you haven't heard that one before." Her smile broadened at him.

"Ah! Yes! I have heard it before. It is still funny. Thank you, Mary. Yes!" He turned to smile directly at her. His teeth glistened white at her.

"I'm starting to think *you're* funny," she said chuckling at him.

"Mary!" he said as his face took on an exaggerated surprised expression. "I hear happiness in your voice again. Yesss."

"OK, I get it," she told him. "The joke wasn't for you. It was for me."

"Yesss," he answered. "Yes, the joke was for you, Mary. I am only happy if you are happy. I like to be happy, so the joke was for you. Yesss."

"You're a nice man," Mary told him.

"Yesss. Thank you, Mary. Yesss." He tapped her leg again with his cane. "So, tell me, what is next for you and your Adam?"

"I don't know. I thought he was going to give me divorce papers last night, but he didn't. It felt more like a date. I slept a lot better last night, and I had dreams about Adam."

"That is good, Mary. Yesss. I am glad to hear it. What will *you* do next?"

She thought for a moment. "I don't know," she answered. "Maybe I'll ask him out on a date."

"Yes, Mary. Date your husband. But let me warn you: Do not try and fix anything. You let God take care of that. Yesss. If you want it fixed, then let God fix it. And I must tell you, God will fix it, but it may not look like what you think you want it to right now. You must be willing to let God mold everything into what He wants. Yesss."

"OK," she replied. "I'll try not to fix it. But how will I know if it's me trying to fix it or if it's God making things happen?"

Allie reached out his hand to her, and she took it. He faced her with his eyes closed. "Mary, you will know. Yesss. You will know. Always ask. Always ask." He continued to hold her hand as he turned and faced forward toward the door. "Man seeks but does not find. He wanders but does not travel. He calls out but does not listen. He hears but does not learn. If man should wait, to rest, to listen, man would know that God heals." Allie tapped his cane once on the floor. "Yesss."

"Now who's that a quote from, Allie?" she asked him.

"I do not know, Mary. Perhaps I made it up. Perhaps it was my great grandfather that told it to me, or perhaps it was Shakespeare that said it." He gave her a large smile. "I like you, Mary," he added. "Yesss."

"I like you, too. I'm glad we met."

Allie began to say 'yes' again, but Mary intentionally tried to beat him to it. The result was that they both said "yes" at the same time in the same drawn out hissing sound. Smiling, Allie turned to face her. A broad smile extended across Mary's face. "Yes, Mary," he said softly as he grinned at her. "Yesss."

Ralph Nelson Willett

Chapter 15

Spring seemed to come later than usual. The winter cold seemed to linger too long, and the snow still seemed too deep. Mary hung her coat in the coat closet, pulled off her shoes and put them on a shelf in her bedroom closet. She sat on the edge of her bed and then fell backward onto it, letting her arms stretch out to either side of her. In spite of the cold chill that still ran through her, she felt contented. She closed her eyes and sighed. Everything seemed to be at peace.

She had just returned from dropping the kids back off with Adam at the house after church. Adam had greeted her with a smile and had even invited her in for coffee. She gladly accepted and spent the next hour with him.

Adam seemed quiet today, contemplative. His anger had faded more since their first dinner date back in February. They had dinner out together twice since then. Adam always brought that large envelope with him but never talked about it or tried to give it to her. It seemed he only invited her out to dinner to give it to her but always changed his mind at the last moment.

Today, over coffee, they talked about the new church that she had been attending the last few months. It was much different than the one they attended together before the separation. The kids liked going to church with her and had even asked Adam if they could attend their mother's church every week. Adam had refused, but he had not been angry about it.

Mary tried to explain to him how she felt about her church. She found it difficult since she was still growing in her faith. All she could tell him was how they had accepted her, brought her in and made friends with her. They had welcomed her and included her even after they knew what had happened between her and Adam. She had told them the whole truth and rather than condemning her they asked how they could help her; what did she need, what could they do?

Adam had at first objected to the children attending Mary's new church. She had pressed him to try to understand what the problem was but it was something he could not define. It took a couple of weeks for her to wear down Adam's resistance, but after giving him a copy of their statement of faith, he never objected again.

This time when they talked, Mary tried to describe the differences between the church Adam attended and the one she attended. She knew Adam's church well and was still learning more about her own. The music was different. Adam's church only sang the old hymns. The only instruments allowed were an organ and a piano. Her church had a full band: drums, guitars, keyboards and four singers. They played contemporary music with a strong beat and uplifting messages of praise.

But the one thing she had the most difficult time trying to explain to Adam was that her church was "alive." Adam's church was not. Adam objected strongly to that characterization. He insisted his church was "alive." She thought she had offended him even though she tried to be careful with what she said. Finally, she said, "Adam, please come and see. Then you tell me if you see a difference or not."

She told him of the Bible studies she had been attending and of the things she had been learning. She could feel her enthusiasm rising as she spoke. Adam listened patiently for a long time then began to pepper her with questions. Because of his earlier studies and desire to go into ministry, he knew much more scripture and theology than she did. He seemed to be looking for ways to challenge her at every point. He was becoming more agitated with every question he asked until Mary said gently, "Adam, come and see. Come and see for yourself and then decide what you think."

Resting on the bed, she began drifting slowly toward sleep. Her mind began to wander wildly and freely. A vision of Allie came to her. He smiled at her with his bright white teeth. He looked at her with those white eyes that seemed empty but happy, blind eyes that saw nothing but at the same time could see deeply into her soul. His face seemed to radiate happiness and perhaps something more. She thought she saw pride in him, pride like a father would have for his children. It felt as if he wanted to wrap his arms around her and tell her that he loved her as if she were his favorite daughter.

Mary snapped fully awake again. She had not seen Allie for a few weeks. She had not been to pray in the chapel. She no longer felt the urgency to use the chapel for prayer but could instead pray where she was, right in her own apartment or sitting at her desk in school. But she missed Allie. Going to the chapel to pray would be her excuse to see him. She rose off of her bed, put her coat and shoes back on and drove to the nursing home.

~~~

Mary saw that Allie's door was closed again. She debated if she should knock and go in but decided she would go into the chapel and pray first. Quiet music was playing through ceiling speakers in the chapel. That was new, she thought. She had not heard music before in here. She listened a moment as an organ played softly. It reminded her of funeral parlor music. It made her uncomfortable. After removing her coat, she sat in her usual chair in the front row. Closing her eyes, she tried to pray, but her mind wandered too quickly. She opened her eyes again and stared up at the cross.

The organ continued to play as her mind aimlessly drifted from thought to thought. Again, the thought of a funeral parlor came to mind as the organ music played. She closed her eyes and tried to understand why this was making her uncomfortable. In her mind, she saw herself standing in the center aisle of a large room with rows of chairs facing forward. At the end of the aisleway was a large dark wooden casket surrounded by flowers. She felt herself walking slowly forward as an organ played softly.

She felt apprehensive as she approached the casket. She knew that there was someone inside, but she did not know who it might be. As she walked forward, she felt a hand take hers. She looked down to see her daughter Kara looking up at her with pleading eyes.

"Don't go, Mommy," she pleaded.

"I have to, Honey," she replied as she released her hand and moved forward.

Another voice called to her from the side of the room. "Mom, please don't," begged Aric.

She stopped to answer him, "I need to." He held out his arms to her with pleading eyes. "It's my fault," she said. "I have to."

She stepped slowly closer to the casket. She stopped at the point where she knew if she took one step further she would see in and know who it was.

"Please no, Mommy," came Kara's pleading voice. She turned slowly to look over her shoulder and saw Kara holding Aric's hand several steps behind her. They had tears running down their faces. "It wasn't you," Kara said.

Unable to pull back, she turned forward again, closed her eyes and took one step forward and stopped. The organ continued to play quietly. Without opening her eyes, she took a second step, paused and listened to the music.

Once more her daughter pleaded. This time she did not turn to look at her. The music stopped abruptly causing her to open her eyes. She peered into the waxy face of Adam lying peacefully at rest. His body was shrouded in brown, withered rose petals. His hands were posed clasped together over his chest holding a live red rose. The rose appeared to be glowing a brilliant red with life. It grew twice its size before her eyes. She gasped and took one step back.

"Two short and one long," said Allie startling her out of her daydream.

Mary stood quickly to turn and face him. She gasped trying to catch her breath. "What?" she asked him breathlessly.

"Two short and one long," he said again. "I heard the train today. Yesss."

"Allie, you frightened me," she told him as she instinctively placed her hand over her heart.

"Yesss, Mary. Why did I frighten you?" He began moving toward the front up the short aisleway of the chapel to meet her. He approached as he tapped his cane from side to side against the chairs.

"Because I didn't hear you come in. You need to make some noise or something, so you won't scare me."

"Perhaps I did, Mary. I believe I said, 'Two short and one long' as a way to announce myself. Yesss."

"No, I mean you should knock or something."

Allie sat down on a front row chair, and Mary joined him. He lifted his face up toward the cross as if it were the sun and he was letting it warm him. Mary lifted up her face in the same way. They sat in silence.

"Where were you, Mary?" Allie asked without turning away from the cross.

"Home. I just got here," she said. "I'm sorry that I haven't come by in so long."

"No, Mary. That is not what I mean. Just now, you were here, but you also were not here. Yesss. Where were you when I came in, Mary?" he asked again.

Mary turned her head to look at him. His blank eyes stared upward toward the cross. She sought words to tell him what she was just thinking. "I was daydreaming I suppose. But how could you know that?"

"Perhaps I can hear it when you breathe or perhaps I can feel your heart as you drift into sadness. Yesss."

"Allie, I don't know how you do that. You seem to know when I come and go and now you know when I'm off daydreaming."

"Yesss."

"How do you do that?" she asked him.

"Where were you, Mary?" he asked again without answering her question.

Mary sighed. "I heard the organ music and I was daydreaming about being in a funeral home. My husband, Adam, was in the casket. His casket was full of dead rose petals. My children were asking me not to go look in the casket, but I did anyhow."

There was silence for a moment. "What organ music, Mary?" he asked.

Mary stopped to listen. The music was no longer playing. "There was organ music playing through the ceiling speakers when I first came in," she told him. "It's not playing now."

"Yesss. I suppose, Mary. Tell me, how did your husband die?"

"He's not dead. I saw him today. He's alive and well. I was only daydreaming about him."

"Yesss. You were dreaming that your husband was dead. Yesss. Is that what you want, Mary? Do you want your husband dead? Yesss." Allie remained facing the cross.

"No. That's not what I want at all."

"Do your children want your husband dead?"

"No. Of course not. Why would you ask that?"

"What did your children say to you in your dream, Mary?" he asked. "Yesss."

"My daughter said it wasn't my fault," she answered. She looked up again to the cross. "It wasn't my fault," she repeated quietly.

"Yesss," he said as he faced her. "it is not your fault. You carry much guilt, but the guilt is not yours. Yesss. Two short and one long. Yesss."

"Yeah, well," she began. "It was just a daydream. I don't know why I went there, but I don't want Adam dead.'

"I was born on Armistice Day. Yesss. Your peace will come. Perhaps it has already come. Yesss."

"Allie, I don't understand you. Does anyone?"

"Yesss."

Mary sat quietly as Allie looked back up at the cross. She followed his blind gaze and looked up with him. "What does that mean, Allie?" she asked him.

"What does what mean, Mary?"

"You said 'your peace will come'," she replied. "What does that mean?"

"Have I said something wrong, Mary? Your voice sounds worried. Yesss," he responded.

She looked at the side of his face as he looked upward. When she did not answer him, Allie turned slowly to face her. Mary began to speak but stopped. A second time she tried to speak and again stopped. She turned and looked down at the floor. Allie turned slowly toward the cross again. Together they sat in silence.

Long moments had passed before Mary spoke again. She bowed her head and gazed vacantly at the floor. "Allie, do you believe in premonitions?"

"Yesss," he answered with his long one-word affirmation.

"Do you suppose I had a premonition about Adam being dead?"

"It was not. Yesss," he answered. He hesitated for a moment and then added, "But perhaps it was something. Be aware that not every message is from God. You must learn to hear *His* voice, Mary. Old things will pass away. New things will come. Do not seek to reveal for yourself what God will reveal in His own time. Your faith must grow. Then you will know. Then you will know. Yesss."

They both sat in contemplation for several seconds before Mary spoke again. "Ya know, I come here because it's quiet and peaceful. I can pray here."

"Yesss."

"But do you think God hears me?" Mary's eyes began to tear. "Because sometimes I still don't think so." Allie turned to face her again as Mary continued. "I come here and pray and ask forgiveness but I still feel so much guilt. I pray and I pray for Him to save our family but I don't see Him doing that. Adam and I talked for a while today, but I really don't see Adam changing his mind. Sometimes I feel like I'm getting closer to God, more so recently, but honestly, I don't think God cares if my marriage fails or if I live or die. Sometimes, I'm even starting to think there is no God."

Mary felt weak. She looked into his face and saw his compassion, an expression she wished she could see in everyone else, anyone else.

"What am I supposed to do, Allie?" she continued. "What am I supposed to do? I feel so confused. I can't help but think that God would want to save our marriage but I just don't see that happening. I even think that Adam still hates me." Mary hung her head and hesitantly added, "Maybe I do want Adam dead. Maybe that's why I can daydream like that. I feel so guilty about it all."

Allie said nothing. He continued to face her. A minute passed, and he tapped her leg with his cane.

"I'm here," she said as she wiped her eyes again.

Allie remained silent. Another minute passed.

Without looking up, Mary asked quietly, "Aren't you going to say 'yes' or something?"

Mary slouched in her chair. Still, Allie remained silent. He held his blind gaze just above her head.

Mary continued, "All my life I've tried to do the right thing but I've been a disappointment to everyone. Yeah... you should have seen my parents' faces when I told them I was pregnant with Aric. *That* was a disappointment. Their little girl getting pregnant before getting married; that was a *real* disappointment. Now with this; having a one-night stand, there's another disappointment. There's nothing I've done that is anything other than being a disappointment to my parents or to Adam." Mary held her eyes to the floor. She thought for a moment then added, "or God."

They sat in silence a few moments longer. Allie waited for her to continue. Another long minute had passed before Mary looked back at Allie. She then asked hoarsely, "What am I supposed to do?"

"Two short and one long," Allie responded quietly. "Yesss."

"What?" Mary asked. His response was exasperating.

"Has Adam asked you for a divorce yet? Yesss," Allie said.

"No," Mary replied.

"God is not far from you. He has sent an angel to minister to you. He has seen your pain and has not forgotten. Do not forget that God uses your suffering and the troubles that come to you to grow your faith. God has planted a seed of faith in you. Yesss. What you think you see as God's silence is God letting that seed grow. You must trust him, Mary. Yesss." Allie reached out his hand to her, and she took it and held it.

"You know, Allie," Mary said. "Sometimes I think you're an angel."

Allie smiled at her with his perfect white teeth. "Yesss. Perhaps I am, Mary. Yesss.

Chapter 16

Mary sat across from Miranda in the coffee shop booth. She had wanted to get together one last time for coffee with her before school began next week. Then they may be too busy to spend much time together. Miranda had become her closest friend since the separation. When Miranda and her husband volunteered to help her move her belongings from the house to her apartment, it had truly been a Godsend. She did not know what she would have done without their help. Since that time, Miranda had introduced her to her new church and to a Bible study she attended during the week. Her entire attitude toward God had changed. Where once she may have doubted that God existed, she now knew that God was alive. She felt as if she were drawing closer to God every day.

"So, what's the news on the divorce?" Miranda asked.

"Nothing yet," responded Mary. "I'm pretty sure he's had the papers for a few months now but just hasn't given them to me yet."

"Do you think he's going to?"

"Probably. Sometimes it seems like he's forgotten about what happened and he's the same old Adam. Sometimes it's more like we're dating again. But other times he seems so angry. I don't know what he's going to do."

"Well I hope he makes up his mind," Miranda responded. "For your sake. Don't drag it out. What's your lawyer say?"

"I don't have a lawyer. I'll get one when he gives me the papers. Until then I'll wait."

"Well don't wait too long. If he's vindictive, he could take everything, including your kids."

"I don't think he'd do that," Mary told her. "He's still a good guy. We're going out to dinner again this weekend. His Mom and Dad are going to take the kids for a while so we can talk. The last few times we went out it was good."

"I'm praying for you, Mary," Miranda said. "I can only imagine what you're going through."

"Please, Miranda," Mary said. "I really don't want to think about it right now."

"OK. I'm sorry. I didn't mean to make you uncomfortable," Miranda told her.

"You're fine," Mary said. "Thank you for praying for me. It's just I'd like to focus on happy things for a while." Mary looked around the cafe as if trying to find a better subject. She turned to Miranda and said, "Have you ever heard that train whistle? I keep hearing it, but no one can tell me what it really is."

"What whistle?" Miranda responded.

"Every once in a while, I hear a train whistle. I hear it almost every day now. It almost sounds like it's getting closer. It blows two short whistles and one long. I only know one other person that says he's heard it."

"I've never heard a train whistle," Miranda told her. "It can't be a train. There aren't any around here."

"Yeah, I know that. But that's what it sounds like." Mary began to sound enthusiastic. "I've heard train whistles before. I'm thinking maybe somebody has some type of steam engine that they're playing with, some guy's hobby. I just wish someone else would hear it so I wouldn't be thinking that I'm crazy."

"You said someone else has heard it, too, so you can't be too crazy," Miranda said as she grinned at her.

"Yeah, but he's an old man. He's got to be around a hundred years old. And he might actually *be* crazy," Mary replied as she grinned back. "'Two short, one long.' That's what he keeps saying. 'Two short, one long'."

Miranda thought for a moment. "Those train whistles used to mean something. It's probably a signal of some type. Figure out the signal, and maybe you'll figure out where it's coming from; probably a factory or something. And I think I know somebody that could tell us exactly what the train whistle signal means if that's what it is."

"Who?" Mary asked.

"My brother. He's a train nut. Knows everything about them. If anybody knows, it's him." Miranda pulled her cell phone from her purse. "I'll call him."

"Oh no, don't do that. It's not that important."

"It won't take but a second," Miranda said as she dialed her brother.

Miranda's head popped up, and she grinned at Mary indicating he answered. "Yeah? Do you greet everyone like that?" She listened into the phone then added, "OK, you can stop now. Hey, I've got a train question for you. What does a train whistle mean when it's two short and one long?"

Miranda's smile broadened as she listened. "Hold on. I need you to tell that to my friend, Mary. Here, tell her what you just told me." She handed the phone off to Mary and said, "This is my brother, Jim. I *told* you he'd know."

Mary took the phone hesitantly and put it to her ear. "Hello?" she said into it.

"Hi, Mary," came Jim's voice through the phone. "So, you want to know what a train whistle means? Two short and one long?"

"Yeah," replied Mary. "Does it mean anything?"

"That's called the 'God Whistle' or sometimes the 'Preacher Whistle,'" Jim said. "Back in the old days, not every town had a minister that lived there. Traveling preachers used to go from town to town. They rode the trains when they could. They'd stay in a town for a couple of weeks and then move on to the next town."

Mary looked up at Miranda with a grin. Jim continued, "The story goes that the engineers on the train would blow two short and one long as a warning just before getting to town. It was a signal that basically told the people to clean up their act real quick because the preacher was coming. The town always wanted the preacher to think that they were always good, clean, Christian people, so they'd hurry up and hide anything they thought the preacher wouldn't like."

"They also said God came with the preacher," Jim continued. "If the town was having some kind of trouble, they'd look forward to when the preacher got there because they thought God would fix everything. So it got to be called 'the God Whistle' because God was coming to fix things, to make things better."

Mary remained quiet as she thought about what she just heard.

"Hello?" asked Jim.

"Yeah, I'm here," Mary told him.

"I thought I lost you for a second."

"No, I'm here. I'm just surprised, that's all."

"So why do you need to know about the God Whistle?"

"Well, because I keep hearing it," Mary told him.

"Where?"

"Here in town."

"In River Run?" Jim asked with a surprised voice.

"Yes."

"There aren't any trains anywhere around River Run. Haven't been in decades. There aren't even any tracks in town anymore. You can't be hearing a train whistle."

"I know," responded Mary. "But that's what it sounds like."

"I've never heard it."

"Are you in town?"

"Yes. Well, I live just outside of town. I think I'd hear a train whistle if there were one in River Run. I've never even heard anything that sounds anything like a train."

"Well, I'm not crazy," Mary said defensively. "I've heard a whistle. I think it's getting louder."

"Well, if you ever figure out what it is, let me know because now I'm interested. Who would be blowing the God Whistle?"

"Alright, I'll let you know if I find out. Here's Miranda again." Mary handed the phone back to Miranda.

Miranda thanked her brother and disconnected the call. "You looked confused," Miranda told Mary.

"I feel like it," Mary said. "Why am I the only one that hears it? Who knows, maybe I am crazy."

"You know you're not crazy," Miranda said as she smiled at her. Mary did not return her smile. "It's probably just somebody screwing around. You'll figure it out."

Chapter 17

Mary sat at Rhonda's kitchen table sharing a cup of coffee with her. The sky had turned dark as the storm moved in making noon seem like late evening. A cold fall wind blew the rain hard against the windows, obscuring any view of the outside world.

"Wow," Rhonda said. "I'm glad I don't have to go out today."

Mary only nodded as she watched the rain pelting the windows. She had walked to Rhonda's apartment from hers only minutes before the rain started. Now it looked like she was going to be trapped here awhile.

"How are the kids doing?" Rhonda asked.

Mary shrugged. "Good," she said. "Aric likes his new teacher. Kara can't wait until she gets to go to school.

You've seen her reading her books. She'll be way ahead of the rest of the class when she starts kindergarten next year."

Rhonda was quiet for a moment, then said, "I can't believe that it's been almost a year now."

Mary looked at her questioningly. "What's been almost a year?"

"Since you and Adam separated."

Mary blinked at her a couple of times. "You're right," she said. "I hadn't thought of that."

"And Adam still hasn't asked you for a divorce," Rhonda stated matter-of-factly as she shook her head.

Mary shook her head and smiled. "That's a good thing. There's still hope until he does. I'm still hoping for reconciliation."

"You know," Rhonda said. "I'd almost have to say that it's been good for you."

Mary tilted her head at her sister. "What do you mean?"

"Well, look at you," Rhonda answered. "You're different. You're calmer or something, more at peace. I don't know."

"Ah," Mary grinned back. "I guess a bit of prayer might do that to you."

Rhonda chuckled. "Prayer," she said. "Sure."

"No, I'm serious," Mary protested.

"Yeah, I know. But you haven't been to the chapel in a couple of weeks."

Mary looked down at the table. "Yeah, I feel kind of bad about that. I like to, but I haven't found that I need to be in the chapel to pray. I can do that wherever I am now."

"OK," Rhonda said. "But you have to admit you *are* different somehow."

"Yeah," Mary admitted. "I'd have to say that my new church has a lot to do with that. I mean, you and I grew up in church. You don't go anymore, but I've pretty much always gone to church. But now I almost feel like all that time I spent in church before, I was just pretending."

"Pretending?" Rhonda asked.

"Yeah. I'm not sure how else to put it. I went to church and did church things, but now it feels like I didn't know God at all. I just pretended that I did. It's different now. At my old church, we all just did what I'd call 'churchy things'. It wasn't real or maybe I should say that looking back it never felt real. You know what I mean? Not like now. My new church showed me Jesus in a way I never knew before. I know Him and I know He knows me. I trust Him now."

"I can see you've changed," Rhonda said as she nodded her head.

Mary leaned back in her chair and looked at Rhonda quizzically. "I never did ask you what turned you off from church. What happened?"

"Something happened in college. I never told you."

"What?"

"Nothing really bad or anything," Rhonda said. "It seems dumb now. I was dating a guy, and we were going to his church. Then he broke up with me."

"That's it? You broke up with a guy, and so you stopped going to church?"

"I know, it sounds kind of silly, but I was mad at him and mad at God and then I figured that because the guy dumped me like he did, and he was supposed to be a Christian, that there wasn't a God. I started questioning everything."

Mary looked at Rhonda somewhat puzzled. "Why would that make you think that there wasn't a God? "

"I know, it seems kind of silly now. I get it. But when you and Adam separated, didn't that make you question if there was a God or not?"

"No. Not really," Mary answered. "When Adam threw me out and I went to the chapel in Forsythe, I just prayed and asked why? I asked God to fix my marriage.

It didn't make me believe that He didn't exist. I had to believe in God. If anything, it made my faith stronger. And you know, it's alright to question Him. I think God understands that and wants to help us through all that."

"Right," Rhonda replied without trying to hide her sarcasm. "I know you've been praying for you and Adam to get back together again. I don't see that happening. If there's a God, then it looks like He's hands off. I'm thinking that you just being alone for a while has made you a better person. Not so much because of God."

"I actually stopped praying for God to restore my marriage a long time ago."

Rhonda looked surprised. "But you said you're still hoping that you two will reconcile."

"Yes. That's true. I'd like to be a family again. But now what I'm praying for is that what God wants to happen, will happen."

Rhonda squinted at her. "That sounds like you've given up."

"No, I haven't. I do tell God that I'd like to have my family back together again. But I'm asking God what He wants now because I think that's more important than what I want. Like I said, all that time I was going to church before I felt like I was just pretending. I never really prayed at all. When we separated, then I only prayed because I was desperate. I'm not desperate now.

I'm trusting now. I think God has a plan and now I want to see what it is."

"That is if there is a God," Rhonda said.

"I know you quit believing a long time ago. It wasn't until I started going to my new church that I really started believing for real. Everything I did before was out of habit until I needed something more. I found that 'more.' I know there is a God. Better yet, I know God and I know He knows me. If I'm different, then it's because of Him. I've learned a lot. Now I want what God wants because I know it will be better. I hope He wants Adam and I to get back together but if not then I'm OK with it, I suppose."

"You suppose?"

"Yeah. I know I'll be alright."

Rhonda looked at Mary over her coffee cup as she took a sip. "Yeah," she said. "I think you *will* be alright."

"I do feel different now," Mary said. "It's different when you really have Jesus in your life and aren't pretending anymore." Mary took a sip of her coffee then grinned at Rhonda. "And Adam still hasn't asked me for a divorce yet."

"I wish I could have been as calm as you when I was going through the break up with my husband," Rhonda told her.

"I wish you could have, too," Mary replied. "It's not too late. Why don't you come to church with me this Sunday?"

Rhonda thought about it for a minute. "You really *are* different," she said. "You've never asked me to go to church with you before."

"Yes, I know," Mary said. "I should have asked you sooner."

Rhonda nodded slowly as she thought about it. "Alright," she answered. "I know your new church isn't like your last one. I didn't like that one at all. There was nothing there that made me think that God was real. Let's see if your new church can convince me.

"Trust me on this, Rhon," Mary said with a smile. "God is real. He is *very* real."

Ralph Nelson Willett

Chapter 18

Mary heard the whistle, two short and one long blast. It was close, *very* close. She stood on the train platform and let her eyes follow the tracks until they curved out of sight behind the trees. Aric and Kara were both excitedly running to the end of the platform and then back again to her.

"He's coming!" Aric shouted to his mother. He jumped up and down as an eager energy burst from him.

"He's coming!" Kara shouted mimicking her older brother.

Again, the train whistle blew two short and one long blast. Kara ran up to her mother and wrapped her arms around her legs. "He's coming!" she said as she beamed up at her.

Aric was dressed in a dark suit, a bright tie, and shoes that were polished to a bright shine. Kara wore a dress that matched her mother's in every way. Their white flowered calico dresses flared out in ruffles and lace. Kara's bright white shoes clacked loudly on the wooden planks of the train station platform as she ran giddily back and forth.

"What is this?" Mary asked aloud as she began to see white smoke puffing skyward above the trees.

Adam stepped up beside her and took her hand. He was dressed in a dark suit. He tilted his head up slightly as he looked down the tracks with a bright smile on his face. "He's coming," Adam said. "He's going to fix it."

"Who's coming?" Mary asked. "Fix what?"

A twenty-piece marching band in full red and white uniforms marched out of the train station and lined up stiffly on the platform facing the direction of the incoming train. They held their instruments out in front of them with their left hand, and they placed the back of their right hand in the small of their backs. Their tall hats obscured Mary's view of the end of the platform where Aric excitedly paced, ran and jumped back and forth.

Again, the whistle blew, two short and one long. It was much closer now.

As the train rounded the curve into view she heard Aric screaming "He's here! He's here!"

The steam locomotive was decorated in purple and white flags. Gold and chrome fittings sparkled brightly in the sun against the backdrop of the polished black paint of the locomotive. It chuffed loudly and squealed as the brakes were applied. It slowed the closer it came.

The band struck up a loud marching song. Trumpets, trombones, flutes, and drums all played a grand welcome.

"He's here," Adam said calmly. Mary looked up into his face. "He's going to take care of it now." He had a peaceful smile as he lifted his head trying to see over the tall hats of the band members.

The train station master stepped out onto the platform and stood next to Adam. Mary could see him smiling behind his thick beard. He pulled out a pocket watch, opened it and checked the time. "He's right on time," he said. "Just like always. He's never late." He tucked the watch back in his vest pocket. "Everything's gonna be alright now."

"Who is this?" she asked Adam loudly over the band.

Mary saw two passenger cars as the train engine and coal car rolled slowly past her chuffing loudly. The first car was a dark forest green. It was polished to the point that Mary could see her reflection in its paint. The second car was white, adorned with more gold and silver. A purple cloth was woven through the silver railings on the front of the car. It had small purple flags that extended at an angle upward from the rails. From where Mary stood, she could see that the rear of the car had a small platform. Its railings were woven through with purple and white cloths. Two large flags angled outwards and up. One was purple and the other white. They waved lazily in the breeze.

The locomotive made a loud hissing sound as the first passenger car screeched to a halt beside them. The last passenger car stopped at the end of the platform. As the train came to a halt, it sounded the whistle one last time, two short and one long note that extended for several seconds. A loud cheer broke out. The band broke formation and crowded the end of the platform with a hundred other people to greet whoever it was that was coming out of the second car onto the end of the platform.

"He's here!" Adam said excitedly as he tugged her hand trying to pull her along with him towards the crowd. Mary looked at Adam confused. "Come on!" Adam said with the brightest smile she could remember him ever having. He released her hand and waved her forward as he ran to join the crowd pressing toward the end of the platform.

A man dressed in a sharp suit stepped up beside her from behind. The suit was dark, neatly pressed with creases and a bright blue silk tie. A matching silk handkerchief was sticking out of the breast pocket. Two golden rings with diamonds that sparkled in the sunlight adorned each of his hands.

The man turned his head to face her. Mary recognized him immediately. It was Allie. He was a young man and no longer blind. He looked to be about thirty-five.

His eyes were almost iridescently blue, unnaturally bright. He smiled kindly at her and nodded his head in a silent greeting. The noise of the cheering crowd faded to silence even though she could still see that they were still cheering and the band still played their instruments. "He's here now," he said calmly. "The time has come to take care of it."

"What?" Mary asked. "Who's here?"

Allie did not answer. His smile broadened, and he turned and walked calmly to the front passenger car. He stood on the bottom step of the car, turned to face her again and in a soft, peaceful voice said, "I was born for you on Armistice Day. My job is finished now." He nodded towards the crowd. "He came for you, but He has *always* been here, Mary. He has always been here." He took the second step up then stopped again. His bright eyes looked deeply into hers. "Yesss," he said. He paused as he smiled at her, waved and climbed into the train car out of her view. The noise of the crowd returned.

Mary awoke from the dream slowly. The band music and cheering crowd faded from her ears as she became aware of where she was. She lay on her side with her head resting comfortably on her pillow. She remained there several minutes as she played the dream over again in her memory. Rolling over onto her back, she asked out loud quietly, "Who's coming? Who's here?"

Ralph Nelson Willett

Chapter 19

Adam watched Kara playing with her dolls on the living room floor. He was half-heartedly trying to read a book. He felt weak, cold, and for some unknown reason, he felt uneasy. He could not shake the feeling that he was sinking. He tried to remain focused on the book but struggled to keep his mind from wandering. He was going to have to make dinner soon but did not think he had the energy for it. Pizza was sounding good again, a quick phone call and dinner would be on the table in thirty minutes.

He noticed his hands were trembling. He became aware he felt nervous about something but had no idea what was bothering him. Perhaps it was just exhaustion that he felt. He closed his eyes and tried to relax.

He thought about calling Mary and arranging to hand off the kids tonight. He could take them over to her apartment along with the pizza, and then he could come home and try and catch some extra sleep.

Adam pulled out his cell to check the time. As he opened its case, it vibrated with an incoming message from his coworker, Jacob Marenisco. He read it. "Have you seen the news?"

He sent a text back "No. What news?"

Moments later another text from Jacob arrived with only a single web page link. He opened it and began to read it. His trembling became more pronounced. He felt his entire body shake. He cast the phone to the sofa cushion and let out an "Ohhhhh" as he buried his face in his hands. A cold chill ran through his body causing a single shiver to shake him involuntarily. His eyes began to tear.

Kara looked up at him, becoming frightened and confused. She stood and moved to stand in front of her father. She reached out both hands and placed them on his knees. "Daddy?" she asked. Adam looked down to see his daughter's frightened eyes looking back at him. He reached down and picked her up and hugged her tightly. The frightened girl began to cry quietly with him.

"It's OK, Kara," he told her. "It's OK. Daddy's just sad. I'm sorry. It's OK." He rocked her back and forth to console her as well as himself. "I'm so sorry, honey. I'm so sorry." He tried to get himself under control again. He held Kara tightly as he suppressed his tears.

"Daddy?" the little girl questioned with tears in her own eyes as she looked at her father.

"It's OK, Kara. Daddy doesn't mean to cry. It's OK."

Kara leaned back to see his face. Tears ran down Kara's cheeks. She reached up and brushed them away then she reached in and gently wiped the tears from her father's cheeks. "Why are you crying, Daddy?"

Adam sought words that he could use to explain to his daughter, just barely four years old, something he was not sure he understood himself yet. "I'm sorry, honey. Daddy messed up, and now he's got to go try and make it better."

The little girl brushed his tears again and then leaned in and kissed him on the cheek. "Does that help, Daddy?"

"Yes, Honey," he answered weakly. "Yes, it does help. Thank you."

"You're welcome, Daddy."

Adam hugged her again and held her tightly for a moment and then stood with her in his arms. "We have to go see your Grandma," he told her as he set her down on the floor. He looked around wildly trying to think of what he needed to do to take the kids to his mother's house. He changed his mind and pulled out his phone. When his mother answer he said, "I need you to come over for a little bit."

"What's going on?" asked his mother.

"I'll have to explain later. Right now, I have to go somewhere, so I need you to watch the kids for a few."

"Now?"

"Yes, please," Adam pleaded.

"Alright. I'll be there in a couple."

"Thank you," he told her.

He disconnected the call and returned to the news web page that Jacob had sent him. He heard the printer in his office as he printed out the article. He retrieved the paper and sat down with it at the kitchen table. He cried again as he reread it. Putting the paper on the table in front of him, he folded the paper in half, folded his arms over it and rested his head on his arms. Tears rolled down his cheek slowly as he blinked them away. "I'm sorry," he whispered to no one.

Minutes later his mother arrived, and he met her at the door. She could see he had been crying. "What's wrong?" she asked him.

"I'll have to explain later. The kids need to eat. Thanks, Mom." He rushed into the garage and to his car.

~~~~

Adam knocked on Mary's apartment door and waited nervously. He paced back and forth in front of the door as he tried to think of the words he would need to say.

No answer. He knocked again, and still, there was no answer. He was not sure if he was disappointed or relieved as he sat on the bottom step of the stairs to wait.

He let his eyes go unfocused as he stared forward. The news article ran through his mind over and over. Tears welled up again. He brushed them away and sniffed. He noticed that his hand trembled as he held the rolled-up printout. He glanced at it, unfurled it and reread the first paragraph. He looked away again. It had been almost a year. His eyes began to tear as the year played out in his mind; the wedding, the one-night stand, his anger. Remorse flooded through him.

He leaned against the stairway railing and waited. He did not know when to expect Mary to come home. He did not know if he should wait for her here, call her, or go home and come back later. His mind raced too quickly for him to decide.

Ten minutes passed. It felt much longer. Adam finally stood and began walking slowly up the stairs with his hand lightly brushing the stair railing. He turned the corner at the first landing and came face to face with Mary. They stood a moment looking at each other. Adam moved his mouth to speak, but nothing came out. His face paled.

"What's wrong?" she asked.

Adam only stood staring at her as his eyes welled up again with tears. He moved his mouth to speak, but again nothing came out.

"What's wrong?" Mary asked again, becoming worried.

Adam turned slowly and began walking back down the stairs to her apartment door. Mary hurried to walk beside him. She began to feel a panic. "Are the kids OK," she asked worriedly. "Where are the kids?"

"They're fine," he said in a choked whisper. "They're with my mom."

"What's wrong?" She saw the paper he was holding in his hand. "What is it? What's wrong?"

"Let's go inside," he told her as he wiped his eyes.

Mary let him into her apartment. The knot in her stomach tightened. She set her purse down on the table and asked him again, "What's the matter?"

Adam looked pale and frightened as he slowly held the rolled paper out to her. She quickly took the paper from him and began reading. It had taken only a moment before she looked up at Adam again.

Tears began to stream down Adam's face. "I'm so sorry," he whispered. "I am so sorry." He struggled with each word.

Mary's mouth hung open as she realized the implications of what she was reading. She looked at the paper and continued reading. The news article reported that Gabriel Anthony Fellows had been caught putting date rape drugs into a woman's drink. After being arrested, he confessed to being a serial rapist. Authorities were attempting to contact the victims.

She looked up again into Adams' face. "I was raped," she said as she tried to wrap her mind around it.

"I'm so sorry," Adam said again. "I am so sorry." Adam appeared to be crumbling into himself.

"I was raped," she repeated to him with more strength.

Adam nodded. "Yes," he whispered.

Mary's eyes darted around the room as she considered everything.

"Yes," Adam said again. "I am so sorry." Tears streamed down his face as he watched Mary's reaction.

Mary struggled to take it all in. "He raped me," she said as she sat in a kitchen chair. "He stole my life."

"I am so sorry," Adam whimpered. "I didn't know. Please forgive me. I am so sorry."

Tears began to stream down Mary's cheeks as well. "He raped me," she said again. "It wasn't my fault. He raped me."

"No, it wasn't your fault," Adam responded. "It was my fault. I'm the one to blame. I am so sorry."

They remained silent as Mary tried to understand it all. She looked up at Adam. He stood in front of her looking guilty and ashamed. "What do we do now?" she asked him.

Adam wiped his face on his sleeve. "I don't know. I've caused so much pain. I don't know what to do now."

Mary stood and pulled a tissue from a box on the counter. She wiped her face with it and then offered the box to Adam. He took a tissue and wiped his own eyes and nose.

"He did this to us," Mary said as she leaned back against the counter. "He did this to us." She looked at Adam who nodded his head. "What do we do now?" she asked again.

"I want to fix this," Adam said. "I am so sorry."

"Yeah, me too," she replied. "But I don't think I know how."

"Me neither," he answered in a hoarse whisper.

"It's been a year."

"Yes. I am so sorry."

They stood in stunned silence, both of them looking down at the floor. Finally, Mary told him, "I'd like to be alone now."

"OK," he replied. "I am so sorry. Please forgive me."

"Thanks for letting me know, Adam." She looked up at him. "We'll talk later. Right now, I need to be alone."

"OK," he said again as he turned and opened the door. He turned one last time to face her before he stepped out. It appeared as if he was going to say something more but then lowered his head, shook it sadly and left the apartment.

Mary stared at the closed door for some time. She poured herself a glass of water and sat down with it on the edge of the sofa. Holding the glass with two hands, she stared into the water. Sadness overwhelmed her. She began to sob. She put the glass on the end table, put her face in her hands and wept.

For an hour she alternated between weeping, crying softly and letting her mind race in many different directions. Nothing made sense, and at the same time, this painful news made sense of it all. She had been drugged and raped. That's all there was to it. She had thought she had brought this on herself by drinking to the point of losing control. Now, after a year, to find that someone she knew had drugged her and took advantage of her did not make things any easier. Her marriage to Adam had been ruined. So much had been lost. So many angry words had been exchanged. So many scars had been created that would never go away. Her only prayer now was simply to ask: "Why, God?"

She wanted to talk with someone, anyone but felt too alone. She had lost so many friends she could think of no one left she could pour her heart out to. Miranda came to mind. She reached for her cell phone but then changed her mind. She was not sure why she held back, but something in the back of her mind told her not to.

She closed her eyes and said a small prayer out loud. "Father, I don't know what to do. Please show me what to do."

She sat up again on the edge of the sofa and stared out of the apartment window toward the playground. The sun had not yet fallen over the horizon and sunlight still shone brightly on the floor. She stood, stepped to the window and rested her hands on the sill. As the warmth of the sun soaked in, she closed her eyes and faced into the light.

An image of Allie came to mind, and she felt a sudden urge to see him. It had been almost a month since she had last gone to the chapel to pray. She felt a pang of guilt for not going to see Allie. He was someone who never seemed to judge her through all this. The one person she could talk to when she needed it the most. She decided she would go to see him. He could be someone that could help her process through this.

~~~

"Hi, Mary," Rhonda greeted as she saw Mary coming down the hall. "You're here early today."

"Yes," she answered as she hurried by. "I need to see Allie."

"Who?" Rhonda asked.

"Allie Blunt," she answered as she walked past. "The guy across the hall from the chapel."

"What guy across from the chapel?" she asked, nearly shouting at her as Mary rushed down the hall. "There's no one across from the chapel."

Mary stopped and turned to look at Rhonda. A feeling of dread came upon her. Had Allie passed away in the month she had not seen him? Rhonda hurried to join her.

"Yes, there is," Mary insisted. "That old guy who keeps saying 'yes' all the time."

"I don't know who you're talking about." Now Rhonda appeared confused.

"Come with me," Mary said as she started briskly walking again. Rhonda hurried to walk along side of her.

As they turned the corner of the hall by the chapel, Mary froze in her tracks. She walked slowly to the chapel door and looked in its door window. This was the chapel where she had been coming to pray. There was no doubt. But across the hall, where Allie's room should be, was a solid wall.

Mary looked at Rhonda confused. "There was a room here," she told Rhonda.

"Mary, there's never been a room here," Rhonda told her. "That's an outside wall."

Mary opened the door to the chapel and quickly moved to the table where she had hidden the little envelope inside the Bible. She found it easily. Rhonda stood in the doorway of the chapel. She held her hands together down in front of her. She appeared worried.

Mary began to speak rapidly. "The blind man with the white cane! Allie! His name is Allie Blunt! His eyes are pure white! He's blind!"

"I'm sorry, Mary. We don't have anyone here by the name of Blunt. We don't have anyone like that."

Mary quickly walked past her into the hall and then approached the wall slowly. She placed her hand on the bricks where Allies' door should have been. She swept her hand across it slowly. She turned to look again at Rhonda while keeping her hand on the wall. "There was a door here. I swear."

Rhonda did not know what to say. There was no patient room there and never had been. She could feel her sister's pain. It hurt her to see Mary so confused and troubled.

Mary moved her mouth again to say something but nothing came out. Again, she tried to speak and again could not say anything. Her shoulders slumped as she accepted the fact that there was no door across the hall from the chapel. She hung her head and began walking slowly back toward the exit. Rhonda walked beside her, watching her carefully.

They walked in silence until they were halfway down the hall again. "I'm sorry," Rhonda told her. "Are you OK?"

"I did come in here to pray in the chapel, didn't I?" Mary asked softly.

"Yes. You come here a lot."

"Allie was the only one that heard the whistle too."

"What whistle?" Rhonda asked.

"The train whistle," Mary answer. "Two short and one long. The God Whistle. The one that tells people God is coming."

"I've never heard a train whistle."

Mary stopped, looked at her and blinked a couple of times. "I know," she finally said.

Mary exited the building and walked to her car deep in thought. She opened the driver's side door and stopped to listen. She could hear the wind blowing through the fall leaves. She waited. She strained her ears to hear it, but there was no whistle.

Chapter 20

Mary returned to her apartment. As she set her purse down on the kitchen table, her phone rang inside it. An unfamiliar number with no name displayed as she pulled it out. She answered it. "Hello," she said into it. Her voice was unexpectedly weak. She cleared her throat. "Hello," she said again.

"Have I reached Mary Champion?" said a woman's voice back to her.

"Yes." Her voice was still weak. She cleared her throat again.

"Hi, I'm glad I could reach you. This is Detective Loretto with the Sheriff's Department. I'm sorry to call you so late, but I need a couple of minutes of your time."

"OK."

"I also have to let you know that I am recording this call. Do you understand?"

"Yes."

"Have you seen the news lately?" the detective asked.

Mary understood without being told what the call was about. She wondered if she had the strength for this conversation. "Yes," she said as she sat down at the table. "Is this about Gabe?"

"If you mean Gabriel Fellows, then yes, it is."

"OK." she said weakly.

"Ms. Champion, do you understand that Mr. Fellows has confessed to certain crimes?"

"Yes. I read the news."

"Well, Ms. Champion, I am sorry to say that he has included your name in a list of his victims."

"I understand," she said as she placed her elbow on the table, rested her forehead in her hand and closed her eyes.

"Are you aware of when this happened?" the detective asked.

"Yes," she answered weakly.

"I'm sorry to have to put you through this, but I need to get some information from you."

"OK."

"Can you tell me what happened?" she asked.

"I was raped," she replied.

"Yes, Ma'am. I'm sorry, but I'm going to need more details. I need anything you can remember."

"We were at a wedding reception at the Florentine Reception Hall. I remember him bringing me a drink. I remember getting up to go dance. I really don't remember anything more until the next morning when I woke up in his hotel room."

"Yes, Ma'am. Can you..."

"I thought I was drunk," she interrupted, speaking more quickly and with gathering strength. Her entire body began to tense. "I thought I did this. He ruined my life."

"Yes. I understand, and I am so sorry for what happened to you, and I'm really sorry that I need to ask you these questions. I know it's painful for you."

Mary relaxed again. The detective continued. "Can you tell me what the next thing is you can remember?"

"I woke up in bed with him in a hotel room. I couldn't remember how I got there. I remember my head hurt. I assumed I drank myself into a blackout. I *never* drink like that. Not since I was a freshman in college. Never!"

"Yes, Ma'am. What happened next?"

"He offered me twenty dollars and told me to take a taxi back to my car. I didn't take the money," she told her. "I had no idea where I was."

"Where was your car?" she asked.

"Still at the reception hall."

"What hotel were you at?"

"I... I don't remember. I just remember going to the front desk and asking them to call me a taxi. I just remember how embarrassed I felt and how mad my husband was going to be because I didn't come home that night."

"Thank you, Ms. Champion. I know it's hard," she told her. "I will need to get some paperwork signed from you but don't worry, I can bring them over. I'll call you to set up a time later this week if that's OK."

"Yes. That's OK." Mary paused then said "Detective?"

"Yes," the detective replied.

"What did he give me?"

"It's not possible to say which drugs or a combination of drugs he used on you. He could not remember which drugs he used on which victim. He confessed to using a few different ones. What he did say is that what he liked to use most often was a combination of two drugs. The first one goes by the common name of Ecstasy. Ecstasy would cause you to become euphoric and reduces your inhibitions. One of the side effects would be that you may sweat a lot and you can become dehydrated quickly. The other side effect may be short term memory impairment.

"The second drug was flunitrazepam. You may have heard it called a 'roofie.' This drug renders the victim incapable of resisting. It would also cause memory loss which we can conclude is the probable cause of you being unable to remember anything of that night.

"In reality, of the twenty-two victims we know about, we are fortunate that he didn't kill anyone."

Mary remained silent on the phone as she absorbed the information. "Are you still with me?" the detective asked.

"Yes, thank you," Mary told her.

One last question before I let you go," she said. "Do you remember the date?"

"Yeah, I remember. It was the day my life was ruined. November eleventh of last year."

"Armistice Day," she replied casually.

"What?" Mary asked surprised.

"Oh, I'm sorry. My husband is a World War One buff. He studies it as a hobby, so I sort of pick up on things. That's the day the war ended in Europe."

"Armistice Day?" she asked.

"Yes, Ma'am. I'm sorry," the detective told her. "I shouldn't have mentioned it. It's not relevant."

"OK," she said as the strength in her voice began to fade again.

The detective continued, "If there's anything else you can remember, anything at all, I'd like you to call me, OK?"

"Yes, I will," Mary replied weakly.

The detective gave Mary her phone number. "I'll arrange to come around and get the papers signed. We can put this guy away for the rest of his life. He won't ruin anyone else's life, I promise."

Mary sat feeling stunned as she hung up the phone. "Armistice Day," she said aloud, letting the words fall quietly from her lips. In her mind, she heard Allie as he said over and over again, "I was born on Armistice Day." She had never bothered to look up when Armistice Day was. Now in some way she still did not fully understand, the pieces of some larger puzzle seemed to all fall into place.

Chapter 21

Mary stood looking into the frozen food selections at Walmart. Trying to decide what the kids might like for meals seemed to be getting more challenging. Her preference would have been always to make fresh meals, but her teaching schedule sometimes made it too difficult. This made frozen prepared meals more appealing. She made her selection, opened the freezer door and began reaching in when she heard a voice behind her. She glanced over her shoulder to see Melissa standing off to her side appearing timid and unsure of herself.

"Hi, Mary," Melissa said.

Mary had only seen Melissa once since the wedding, and that was not pleasant. Melissa had confronted her in this same store just a month after the wedding. She had angrily and loudly called her a drunk and a whore. Melissa told her she did not want anything to do with her anymore. Mary had felt so embarrassed and hurt that she had abandoned her shopping cart and run out of the store.

Mary closed the freezer door and gave her a soft smile. "Hi, Melissa."

"Um, I heard what happened," she told Mary. "I mean, I read in the paper what Gabe did and I, um, I just wanted to say I'm sorry."

"Thank you," Mary replied.

"And, um, I just want to say I'm sorry for all those things I said about you. That wasn't right."

"No, it wasn't," Mary said calmly.

Melissa stood nervously in front of Mary, not knowing what to say next. Finally, she said, "Um, OK. It was good to see you again, Mary." She turned and began to step away.

Mary stopped her, "Melissa?" Melissa turned and raised a worried eyebrow. "You know he intended that for you, right?" From the look on Melissa's face, it was evident that she had realized that. "He drugged your beer, and you handed it off to me," Mary said without a hint of accusation.

Melissa stepped closer to Mary. She looked as if she was about to cry. "Yeah, I know," she said softly. "I am so sorry."

Mary nodded sadly. "Do you realize how many friends I lost because of this?" Mary asked her. Melissa looked down without answering. "You're a friend I'd like to keep," Mary said.

Melissa looked up hopefully. "You're not mad at me?" she asked.

"I'm working through a lot of anger. Someone had told me before I knew what really happened that I would have much to forgive. I didn't know what he meant then, but now I do. I think I can truly say that I forgive you and I'd like to restore our friendship."

Melissa looked as if she had not understood but began to brighten as she realized what Mary was saying. She hesitated at first but then moved in to hug Mary. Mary returned the hug warmly. "Thank you," Melissa said as her eyes began to tear up.

"It's OK," Mary told her.

Melissa stepped back. "I've been feeling so guilty since I realized what really happened. They didn't mention who Gabe raped, but I figured it out. I am so sorry," she said as she wiped her eyes.

"I understand," Mary said. "I carried all that guilt with me for months. Now I know it wasn't my fault. And Melissa," Mary said as she reached out and touched

Melissa's arm, "it wasn't your fault either. You didn't do this. Gabe did this."

"But I said some terrible things to you. I am so sorry."

"What you said to me I said to myself a hundred times," Mary said. "I felt the same way about me as you did. If I can forgive me, I can forgive you. You're still my friend, and I love you."

"Thank you," Melissa replied. "I love you, too." Melissa again stepped in and gave Mary another hug. "I love you, too," she repeated.

"Have you got time this week to get together for some coffee?" Mary asked.

"I'd like that," Melissa said. "I'm free every night this week."

"Alright," Mary said smiling. "How about tonight?"

"Sure," Melissa replied. "The coffee shop?"

"Yeah, that would be great. Six?"

"OK," Melissa answered. "I'll see you then."

Melissa gave a wave of her hand, turned and walked away. Mary noticed that she seemed to be walking a little lighter.

Chapter 22

Mary noticed that Adam's hands shook as he sipped from his coffee cup. Even his voice shook when he spoke to her. The waitress had just taken their orders and removed the menus from the table. Now they looked around the restaurant as they each tried to avoid looking the other in the eyes. He appeared more nervous than she felt. The dark circles under his eyes suggested to Mary that Adam probably was not sleeping well either.

Mary had decided that she would let Adam take the lead in this conversation. He had asked her out for dinner, but he did not tell her what he wanted to talk about. She could only guess. Whatever it was, she felt it would be OK, even if he handed her the divorce papers, she thought. It took a long time for him to muster the courage to tell her what he wanted to say.

"I just wanted to say again that I am so sorry, Mary," he said as he tried to face her. His voice trembled. Mary held her reaction in check. She looked into his eyes for a moment until he looked away. He was not strong enough yet to maintain eye contact. "I screwed up," he continued. "I shouldn't have treated you that way."

"No," she replied, "you shouldn't have." She felt surprisingly calm and at peace. She had prayed for wisdom and was now waiting to see how things would play out. She remembered what Allie had said about when God fixes things: they may not look like what she thought they would. She felt that no matter what happened tonight it would be OK.

Adam took a deep breath and then forced himself to look at Mary. "The kids want you to come home."

"I have a *new* home, Adam. They're getting used to things."

Adam's shoulders dropped, and he hung his head. After a moment, he shook his head and said, "I'd like to fix this."

"You can't fix this, Adam," she replied. "I've learned a few things while we've been apart. I've learned that I can't fix things, only God can. What is it that you think *you* can do to fix this?"

Again, he shook his head as he tried to look up at her again. Mary was not sure if his eyes were pleading or just sad. "I don't know," he said. "I don't know what I can do. I don't know what I can say. I've screwed up so badly that I'm not even sure that things can be fixed. I'd like to try."

"You threw me out, Adam," she said calmly. "You threw me out and changed the locks on the doors. I wish things hadn't turned out as they did..." She pursed her lips for a moment and then said, "but they did. I felt guilty for so long. I lost almost all of my friends. I don't think you'll ever trust me again and I'm not sure I'll be able to trust *you*."

Adam wiped a hand down his face and sat back in his seat. He tried to pick up his coffee cup but noticed how it shook and set it back down. "I've learned a lot about myself too, through all this," he said. "I've learned that I don't want to go through life without you. I've learned how much I love you. You mean more to me than I knew. I want to find a way to make it up to you."

Mary narrowed her eyes at him. "What can you possibly think you can do to make it up to me? I was raped, Adam. Then I was thrown out of my home. I lived with a guilt that wasn't mine, and every time I think of you, all I can see is that sneer you gave me when I picked up my things from the house."

"I know," he said as his head drooped again. "I am sorry. It just looked so bad..."

"It was bad," she interrupted. "I was raped." Her voice began to rise in anger. "When I needed you, you were the first one to reject me."

Adam looked up at her. His eyes began to glisten with tears.

Mary spoke more quickly as she continued, "I can't even begin to explain how badly that hurt. There is almost nothing I can remember of that night. I woke up the next morning in bed with a man I hardly knew, and I was terrified. I had no idea what happened. I had no idea where I was. The only thing I could think of was how angry you would be, and you were even angrier than I expected. I thought you were going to hurt me, Adam." She leaned back in her seat and tilted her head. She spoke more slowly to emphasize her point and softly said, "I think you *would* have hurt me if you thought you could have gotten away with it."

Adam wiped a hand over his eyes to wipe away the tears that were forming. He looked around the room. He placed his hands on top of each other on the table, leaned in and looked directly down at them. He bit his lower lip and looked up into Mary's eyes. "Mary, I would never hurt you. Ever. I was angry because of what I thought I knew. What Gabe did, he did to both of us."

Every muscle in Mary's face tightened. 'Did to both of us?' she thought. Rage began to boil inside. She took a deep breath as even her stomach muscles prepared her to scream at him: *'Gabe raped me! You threw me out! You kicked me to the curb!'* A memory of Allie came to mind. She could hear his voice as clearly as if she was in the same room with him again. "Your husband is hurting more than you. He hides his pain behind his anger, but his hurt goes deep." She relaxed again as she released her anger into God's hands. Exhaling with one long controlled breath, she stared at him.

"Perhaps he did," she said calmly. "Yesss." She drew out the 'yes' in the same way Allie had. She continued her stare. He tried to meet her gaze but could not. He kept his eyes facing down at the tabletop. "I'll need some time to think about it," she told him. A spark of hope crossed his face. "But I don't think I want things to go back to the way they were."

Adam appeared confused at that statement. "Wha... what do you mean?"

"Can you honestly tell me you were happy?" she asked him.

"Happy?"

"Yeah. Were you happy with the way things were going, with your job?" she paused for a second then added, "with me?"

Adam pondered the question for a second. "Yeah. I was happy. Weren't you?"

"Adam, you already told me that you weren't happy with our intimate life."

Adam's eyes widened. He opened his mouth to speak and then closed it again. The look on his face told Mary the answer.

"What about your job?" she asked him. "Are you actually happy with that?"

"My job is fine," he said.

"I've had a lot of time to think while we've been apart," she told him. "You wanted to go into ministry. I talked you out of that. That was wrong of me. Now I think you're only working at the credit union because you feel obligated to take care of the kids and me."

"I am obligated," he protested. "That's what I'm supposed to do."

"I'm not so sure," she said. "I spent time talking with someone at the nursing home where Rhonda works. He said we could not run from what God has asked us to do and I think he's right."

"That all changed when we had Aric," he said.

"Did God change His mind? I don't think so. He knew we were going to have Aric. I think He's still asking us to do what He wants. Haven't you felt like you still needed to do that? Haven't you wished you would have?"

"Us?" Adam questioned. "What do you mean by 'us'? That was my calling, not yours."

"Well like I said, I had a lot of time to think about things. I think that once we got married, God's calling for me was connected to yours and yours to mine. And I don't think God has changed His mind about anything. We each still have our own calling but now they're connected."

Adam furrowed his eyebrows as he thought about what she said. "I'm not sure that's my calling. I was ten years younger, and I was a little too idealistic. I'm not sure now that God was calling me to do anything. I think it was just some fantasy in my head."

"Adam," she said. Adam looked up to meet her gaze. "Are you happy?" Adam froze in his seat. Mary could see him thinking over the question.

"Why wouldn't I be happy? We've got great kids, a nice home and I've got a good job."

"Adam," she repeated. "Are... you... happy?"

Adam visibly squirmed, and then his head drooped toward the table. "Sometimes," he began, "I still think about it; going into ministry that is. But I'm not twenty-two anymore. We got pregnant out of wedlock. I'm not fit for any ministry. Plus, there's no way I can afford to go to seminary now and take care of my family."

"Do you think God didn't know what was going to happen? Yes, what we did wasn't right. It was a sin. But God forgave us of that sin, and I don't think He has changed His calling for us. And as far as taking care of our family, is it us who takes care of our family or is it ultimately God? If God wants you to do something then don't you think He'll make a way for it to happen?"

They sat silently for a moment. "What about you?" Adam asked. "Were you happy?"

"No," Mary answered without hesitation. "I wasn't happy, and I'm still not happy."

Adam looked at her guiltily again. "I'm sorry," he said.

The waitress returned to the table with their meals and placed the plates in front of them. They both leaned back in their seats to make room for the waitress to arrange the plates for them. When she left, Mary and Adam stared at their plates.

"Will you say grace?" Mary asked.

"Grace?" Adam questioned. Mary only looked at him. "OK," he said.

Mary could see that he was obviously uncomfortable. She had never known him to say grace over a meal while they were out in public. Adam held out his hand to Mary. She took it and they both bowed their heads while Adam gave thanks quietly to God for their meal.

Mary took her first bite. Adam only stared down at his food. "I'm sorry," he repeated. "I'm sorry I couldn't make you happy."

Mary tilted her head as she looked at him. She swallowed the bite she had taken. "It's not your job to make me happy, Adam," she said. "I've made wrong choices, too. There was a calling by God on my life, and I chose to ignore it, too. So, there we are, both of us refusing to do what God has called us to do and you expect us to be happy?" She took another bite. She still felt calm and even smiled.

Adam did not look up from his plate. Moments passed as Mary watched him. "Mary," he finally said. "I love you. I know I messed up with you and I am so sorry. I was *so* ready to get divorced. I had the papers all ready to give to you, but I couldn't do it. I just couldn't..." His voice trailed off as his throat tightened and began to close in. A tear rolled down his cheek and then another. He made no attempt to wipe them away or hide them. "Pastor Flynn actually advised me to divorce you. I was so confused. It just felt so wrong. Cheryl Fayette approached me right in the church and asked me out. I said 'yes.'" The confessions continued to pour out. "In my mind, I knew what would happen if I went out with her. I knew. But I couldn't do it because I'm still in love with you." Adam's throat was so tight that the last of his words were forced out in a hoarse whisper. The tears flowed onto the table as he hung his head.

"Cheryl Fayette," Mary said flatly as she turned her gaze outside the restaurant window. "That makes sense. She couldn't even wait until we were divorced."

Adam wiped his eyes and cheeks with one hand. Mary reached across the table and placed her hand on his arm.

"Adam," Mary said. "I've always loved you. From the day we first met in college I've loved you. That hasn't changed. I'm sorry I wasn't as intimate with you as much as you needed me to be and that is something I can work on. But I don't want to run from what God has asked us to do anymore. I think we both need to stop running."

Adam wiped his eyes with a paper napkin and set it back down on the table. Slowly he raised his eyes to meet Mary's. "Can we try again?" he asked.

"A few things need to change," she said soothingly. "I can't go back to our old church. Not after they told me not to come back and told you to divorce me. I'm going to a new church now. They've accepted me without question. I've learned so much about God's grace there. I'd like you to come with me."

Adam nodded.

"Secondly, I will support you if you still feel like God is calling you into the ministry. Whatever you choose to do I will be there for you. I can't make you happy, only you can choose to be happy, but I think that if you follow what God is asking of you, you will be."

Adam nodded again and looked at her as if some question had just come to mind. "I haven't been close to God in a long time. I think I may have forgotten what it feels like. Now when I try to pray all I can do is pray for you, that He'll take care of you and that you'll find room in your heart to forgive me."

Allie's words echoed through Mary's mind. She heard him say, "You, Mary. Yesss. I pray for you."

Adam continued, "Now I've got nothing. I've got nothing to offer God, and I don't think He would even want me anymore. If I went into the ministry now and people found out how I treated you and that we were pregnant out of wedlock, what would they think?"

"That's something you need to let God worry about."

"You'd be willing to do what it takes so I can go through seminary?"

"Yes," she answered confidently. "My calling is forever connected to yours."

"What is God calling you to do?" he asked her puzzled.

Mary smiled warmly at him. "I've had a dream since I was a little girl. It's something I've been thinking about a lot recently since I've been living on my own. I even wake up at night thinking about it." Adam looked at her expectantly, having no idea where this was leading. "Adam, I know this is old fashioned, and some people say I shouldn't even be thinking about this at all, but all I want to do is to love you, be your wife and raise our children to be a man and woman of God. What I'm asking to do is to be a stay at home mom to our kids and a wife to you."

Adam appeared stunned. "You want to quit your job?"

"I want a different job. I want the one God called me to do."

"But we'll need your income," Adam said as the implications came to mind.

"What we need, God will provide. We'll do our job, and He'll do His. And there's more. I want to be available to help other couples that are going through rough times. This is what God is calling me to."

Adam visibly relaxed. He used his fork to prod the uneaten burger on his plate. "How did you suddenly become so spiritual?" he asked.

"Because I may have doubted once that there was a God, I don't any longer. He came to town just for me. I heard His whistle, and He sent an angel to help me. If it wasn't for that, I don't think I would have made it."

Adam stared at her. She was speaking in metaphors he did not understand but felt too weak to question.

Chapter 23 Epilogue

Fourteen-year-old Kara Champion had her father wrapped around her finger, and she knew it. She knew she could give him a pouting lip and he would melt. "You must only use your powers for good," her mother would tease her. Kara was moving quickly in an easy jog to try and reach her father and mother before their next couples session began. She found them walking hand in hand just a few paces from the smaller of the Grace Chapel meeting rooms. She bounced up and down in front of Adam.

"Can I have five dollars?" she asked excitedly.

"Five dollars," her father said as he smiled at his daughter's bouncing effervescence. "Why?"

"Cause a group of us are going over to the ice cream shop down the street. Pa-leeease..."

Adam looked at Mary and chuckled. "What do you think?" he asked her.

Mary chuckled back and looked at their daughter. "How about two fifty?"

"No...," Kara whined. "That will only get me a small one."

"Alright," Adam said as he looked at Mary while pulling out his wallet.

"Thank you, Daddy," Kara said cheerily as she took the bill from him. She stood on her toes, leaned in and kissed him on the cheek.

This was a game they had played many times. Kara could easily sweet talk her father into almost anything. Her brothers had to work a little harder to get what they wanted, and her much younger sister was just learning the tricks.

Mary chuckled at him as Kara jogged away just as quickly as she had come. "What?" Adam asked her.

"She has *so* got your number," she told him with a big grin.

"Yeah, probably," he said returning the grin.

Adam held the door for Mary as she entered the meeting room and then let the door close behind them. The chairs were arranged in a circle. Several couples were already seated as they talked among themselves. Mary and Adam chose the seats in front of the white board and began to arrange the handouts they had brought with them on their laps and the chairs to either side of them.

Additional couples joined the circle and Mary did a quick count to see if everyone was there. "Looks like we're missing Judy and Mark," Mary said to the group. We'll give them a couple of minutes before we get started.

As if on cue, the room door opened and another young couple hurried into the room. "Sorry we're late," the woman said as she chose her seat. Her husband sat down beside her. "I tried to get him to drive faster."

"Uh, no," the man said. "Can't blame that on my driving." The woman grinned at him.

"You're not late," Adam told them. "We haven't started yet. But now that we're all here, we can." Adam reached over and held Mary's hand. Most of the other couples in the group followed their lead and also held hands. Adam bowed his head and said the opening prayer.

"OK," Adam said as he took a stack of papers and passed them to his left. "Welcome to week four. Tonight, we're going to have some fun before we break out into our groups." Each person took a sheet and passed it on. "This little test will give us some insights into our personalities, and once we've self-evaluated our own test, our spouses are going to evaluate them and let us know how accurate they are."

The group laughed at the thought of the exercise and comments began to surface from some who were reading ahead. Adam and Mary had been leading this twelve-week marriage enrichment class for Grace Chapel for the last six years. This was their eighteenth time leading different groups through it and each time they had learned even more about themselves. It was during their first twelve-week session that they had an opportunity to announce to the group that they were pregnant with their fourth baby. It would be this session when they would announce that they were now expecting their fifth.

Aric had just passed his second year of Bible college. He enjoyed his baby brother and sisters but was glad when it was time to go back to college. It gave him a much-needed break from his younger siblings. His goal now was to go to seminary and enter the ministry himself, following in his father's footsteps.

Kara radiated beauty, both physically and with her personality. A straight A student, she easily impressed her teachers and counselors. Gifted with intelligence, athleticism, and music, she excelled at everything she did.

Her younger brother could have been her twin were it not for the seven years that separated them. Mary had insisted on naming him Alexander Gregory. They called him Allie.

Rosanne, the baby, was now eighteen months old. She had already earned the nickname "Giggle Monster" because of her penchant for giggling. Rosie brought a smile into every room she teetered into.

Just two weeks ago, Adam and Mary confirmed they were expecting their fifth child. The entire family was thrilled at the prospect of yet another member joining them. Even Aric, who would be twenty-one by the time the baby was born, was happy, albeit equally as happy he would still be away at college.

There had been multiple struggles to reach this point in their lives. Adam began seminary within months of their reconciliation, first online while still maintaining his job at the credit union and then commuting an hour each way four days a week. Mary continued to teach at the Junior High for his first year, then quit to manage their family and home.

Financially it was very difficult. Their savings had dwindled down until they had to decide if they were going to take their final ten dollars out of the bank and close the account or not. They had prayed many times over their finances and it now came down to the decision of which one of them should return to work. They had decided to sleep on it just one more night before making their final decision. God answered their prayers the very next morning. Adam's cell phone rang at almost eight o'clock with a call from Pastor Duane. He said that another member of the church, who wanted to remain anonymous, had felt a special calling from God to support them while Adam went through seminary. From that point on, all of their expenses had been covered; health insurance, car insurance, groceries, and rent. Mary estimated the amount of the gift that had been bestowed on them was more than Adam had been making at the credit union. She never knew who had supported them during that time but asked God to bless them a thousand times greater than their gift had been.

The church they now served was one of the larger ones in town. Adam was an associate pastor. He had found that he was a gifted speaker, but his passion had become helping couples with their marriages. Mary was equally as passionate as her calling intertwined with his. Together they had counseled many families. They helped to guide many couples through the difficult struggles they found themselves in. Many marriages had been saved or restored. Couples who were planning for their marriages sought them out for premarital counseling. Some of them had not been members of their church, but Adam's and Mary's reputation for wisdom and loving, patient guidance preceded them.

Adam had spoken at several churches around the region. His topic had almost always been on protecting marriages. He openly talked about their separation, the counseling that he and Mary had gone through and the struggles they had dealt with. Each speaking engagement seemed to open up two more as he touched lives from all over.

Mary also began to speak at different gatherings. Several women's groups had invited her in to speak. The first request she had was for a small group on a Saturday evening. She had reluctantly accepted. Although Adam had coached her on her topic of strengthening marriage, when she spoke an entirely different story unfolded as the Holy Spirit directed her. It was the story of an old blind man who said she smelled good, laughed at stupid jokes and said 'yes' to everything.

She had found herself in tears as she told the story of the only other person that had heard the God Whistle, "two short and one long." She told them of how he had repeatedly said that he was born on Armistice Day and how she felt when she realized that was the same day as the wedding; the same day she was raped. She ended her story by wondering aloud if she had just made up Aluishous Gregory Blunt. Was Allie a device that her mind invented to deal with her pain or was he literally God's angel? Allie had said, "God is not far from you. He has sent an angel to minister to you." In her quieter moments, she would often wonder if Allie was still watching over her as her ministering angel.

Allie had warned her that when God "fixed" their marriage that it may not look like what she thought it should look like. Now she was thankful that it did not. Without realizing it, she had been unhappy; unhappy in her job, unhappy in her marriage and unhappy in her life. Looking back, she could say, "Of course we were unhappy. It all made sense now." She had been running from what God had asked her to do and had held Adam back from what God wanted *him* to do. Yes, of course, she was unhappy.

But now she could honestly say that both she and Adam were happy. They had both embraced God's calling on their lives. They had trusted Him to enable them to do what He asked them to do. Even with the many challenges they faced, their lives were now both fulfilling and rewarding.

As Mary left the meeting where she had told her story for the first time, the snow was falling in large, heavy wet flakes, muffling the sounds of the night into a peaceful quiet. It pelted her nose and cheeks and gathered on her knitted hat. She left fresh footprints as she crossed the parking lot to her car.

While brushing off the door with her mitten, she heard a distant train whistle. She stopped and turned an ear to its direction. A broad smile crossed her face as she heard it the second time, two short and one long. She stood looking over the roof of her car into the darkness. It was a train that perhaps only she could hear. It caused her to wonder, who the whistle blew for this time. Mary smiled as she thought about it. She then gently kissed the mitten on her hand. "Thank you," she said as she held her hand up to her lips and gently blew the kiss through the snowy night air.

She climbed into her car and put the key in the ignition. She paused before turning the key. She felt a surge of gratefulness swelling up in her. It warmed her against the cold. The memory of Allie as an old blind man came to mind smiling at her with bright white teeth. She remembered a dream, still clear in her mind after all these years. In the dream, she saw Allie as a much younger man with bright blue eyes. She heard him say, "He came for you, but He's always been here, Mary. He's always been here."

"Allie," She said aloud, "thank you, too." She nodded her head as if quietly agreeing with her own thoughts and said, "Yesss." She smiled, started the car, and headed home.

~The End~

Did You Enjoy This Book?

Please follow this link to review it
www.NorthernOvationMedia.com/thegodwhistle/review

Thank you for taking time to read The God Whistle. I appreciate it. If you enjoyed this book, would you please take an extra moment to add a short review on Amazon? Reviews are constructive for authors such as me. They also help to ensure others that this book is worth their time.

Please go to this page:
www.NorthernOvationMedia.com/thegodwhistle/review

Thank You.
Ralph Nelson Willett

Stay In Touch With Ralph Nelson Willett

Stay in touch with the author

Amazon
www. amazon.com/author/ralphwillett

Facebook:
www.Facebook.com/RalphNelsonWillett/

Twitter:
www.twitter.com/northernovation

Email
AuthorRalphNelsonWillett@gmail.com

If you enjoyed The God Whistle, please post a review on Amazon.

Want Free Books?

From time to time Ralph gives away free copies of his new releases. But his promotions are highly temporary. If you'd like to be notified when he's giving his kindle books away for free, please consider signing up at the following link:
www.NorthernOvationMedia.com/freebooks

Other Books By Ralph Nelson Willett

The Release
Escape From Torment

After a lifetime of abuse, Carrie Rhodes attempts to escape but now must hide from her ex-boyfriend and the gang that wants her dead. On the run and just two hours from her greatest fears in Chicago, her car breaks down. With no hope left, she resigns herself to the inevitable.

But hope returns in the form of an extraordinary man with dark secrets and an unusual occupation. For the first time, Carrie finds herself as part of an extended family where love is unconditional and freely given.

However evil refuses to let her go and darkness rages in many forms. Still, Carrie refuses the light that is shining in her life. Can God's love, shown through flawed people, be the path of escape from generations of domestic abuse?

Available on Amazon

The Rose Stone

Rosanne struggles with suicidal thoughts, addiction, and unwanted pregnancy. A small stone, a token from her past, reminds her of the love of her family; a love she once walked away from. In a ruined life and far from home, Rosanne reaches out in desperation for the help she needs. Now a God she rejects reaches into her life through that same small stone, guiding her back home, both physically and emotionally.

The Rose Stone will have you feeling the pain and desperation of a young woman who once had it all but now fights to stay alive. The story takes you in deep as you hear the voices that condemn her, struggle with her as she stumbles and you'll cry with her as she escapes her personal demons. Although it's fiction, this may be a story of someone you know; it may even be you. It's a story of how God can use even the smallest and most common things to rescue a life. In Rosanne's life, it's all touched by a single stone; The Rose Stone.

Available on Amazon

The Summer Tourist

The Summer Tourist - A Contemporary Christian Romance

Tina reflected on how she had been used by the man she loved. The crushing weight of his deception overwhelmed her, leaving only her pain. Standing in front of the lighthouse, she raises tear-filled eyes toward Chicago and whispers, *"I am not your summer diversion."*

She holds the sparkling bracelet he had given her over the water. The final emotional release of letting him go was to turn her hand slowly and let it fall away.

Could she ever trust again? Would an old flame return to love her once more?

The Summer Tourist, A Christian Romance, is set in the city of South Haven MI with its sandy Lake Michigan beaches and iconic lighthouse. As part of the Haven Series, this book examines love and love lost. Can a love and trust ever be restored?

Available on Amazon

Made in the USA
Columbia, SC
30 October 2018